The Great Pebble Affair

THE GREAT PEBBLE AFFAIR

by Brit Shelby

G. P. Putnam's Sons
New York

SBN: 399–11735–0

Library of Congress Cataloging in Publication Data

Shelby, Brit.
    The great pebble affair.

    I. Title.
PZ4.S5432Gr   [PS3569.H39257]   813'.5'4   75–40335

For Brett Petersen and those who know the truth,
laughing all the way

IN THE BEGINNING . . .

I THINK it's my duty to write an account of what happened, I mean what *really* happened, so those of you who are curious won't have to go by the reports in *Time, Newsweek, U.S. News & World Report,* the New York *Times,* the Washington *Post* and *Rolling Stone,* because they're all basically wrong.

I also have been trying to figure out who to blame and maybe writing this will help me to do that. Donnely once tried to explain an idea called existentialism to me. The way I get it, existentialists figure everything is connected pretty much together in one whole and what one thing does goes on affecting everything else, so while you may be responsible for some poor schmuck knocking off his grandmother in Detroit, you're not really responsible because some other poor schmuck ten years ago did something that touched you off into doing whatever you did that touched you off into doing whatever you did that touched off the poor schmuck in Detroit which resulted in him croaking his grandmother. Donnely says the way to look at it is to visualize a pond, a big smooth pond. Then think of somebody throwing a tiny pebble into that pond. The pebble makes ripples and waves which keep on flowing long after the pebble has sunk, one ripple making another and so on. That's what existentialism is, he says. He also says one of the tricks of life is to learn not only how to ride the crests of the flowing ripples, but how to move independently beyond and past their flow.

Of course, I can't really say if that explanation of existentialism is right. I'm just a poor ex-Marine, ex-bank robber, ex-con and multimillionaire corporate tycoon, so I really don't know if that explanation is right. If it is and that's what existentialism is all about, then I think it's a bunch of crap because you can fix blame on people. You just find the clod who threw the pebble in the pond in the first place.

For a long time I thought maybe General Hershey was to blame because he ran the draft and the draft drafted Donnely. Then I thought maybe Ho Chi Minh was to blame because he ran the Vietcong and the NVRs, who I guess were the reason Donnely and I met. But then I decided it was silly (ludicrous, Donnely would say) to blame them, especially since neither of them knew Donnely or I was live. So I've been sifting through the last few years to figure out who is and who isn't to blame.

I date things from that morning in 1968 when our patrol went out to the rice paddies looking for the paratrooper general's pizza copter. It seems an ignorant Vietnamese peasant, ungrateful for the manifold napalm blessings bestowed on his country by Uncle Sam, had thrown some water buffalo dung at the helicopter the paratrooper commander used to ferry the frozen pizzas from Saigon to the paratrooper officers' club. The helicopter, fantastic wingless weapon that it was, dropped from the sky like a stone when the dung got sucked through its electrical system. The crew got away OK, but the paratrooper general was hopping mad because now he would have to divert a copter from another mission to fly in the pizzas. He didn't have the men to spare to retrieve the copter himself, so he asked our commander, who agreed to send a patrol in to see if the copter could be salvaged.

For a while I thought I should blame either the paratrooper general or our commander, but how can you judge a pizza addict or somebody trying to be helpful?

So we went in, a ten-man Marine patrol. We found the copter all right, but we also found a whole battalion of Vietcong. I don't think they were there after pizza, but if they were, they changed their minds when they saw us.

You ever try to run through elephant grass? Don't. Now I

8

know why they make elephants so big and strong: It's so they can run through their grass. There we were, ten scared silly Americans trying to break track records in grass so tall you couldn't see over the tops and so thick you had to part blades to stick a hair between them. Behind us the VC were setting up a machine gun to rake the elephant grass and our poor bodies.

But our luck held. The paratrooper general, anxious to know the fate of his food ferry, sent a reconnaissance copter and a gunship to check things out. They appeared on the scene just seconds after the first burst from the VC machine gun. The gunship went to work on the VC and the recon copter dove down to pick us up. We were ten happy mothers. Well, we were nine happy mothers.

Mother number 10 was the last Marine to dive into the copter. The pilot, not wanting to risk getting chopped up like a sitting duck, was a little too quick with his liftoff. Our last man barely grabbed a strut as the copter shot five hundred feed straight up.

There he was, dangling from the belly of a copter cruising at sixty mph. His body angled almost parallel to the ground and it was a cinch that with all that strain on him he couldn't hold on much longer.

So then I did a stupid thing which makes me sometimes think I'm to blame. I had one of the other guys hold onto my feet and I crawled out on the strut. I grabbed number 10's hands just as he lost his hold and jerked him into the copter.

For that little bit of stupidity I got a piece of bronze-plated tin and everything I own today, for the man I jerked into the copter was Daniel James Donnely.

Donnely came to see me that night back at the base camp. He took one long look at me and said, "Thank you. I won't forget you saving my life and I'll do my best to repay you."

I told him to forget it and have a beer. The long and the short of it was that he moved into the spare bunk in our Quonset hut and we spent the rest of our tour together. Donnely, Frank Douglas and me. Of course, Frank got killed, but that comes later in the story.

It seems Donnely was one of the select group of men who had the unique privilege to be drafted into the Marine Corps. The Marines don't normally draft people, but in 1966 they were short of guys like me who for some strange reason volunteer, so they drafted a few.

"There we were," Donnely says whenever he tells the story, "me and this other guy, standing around in our shorts, waiting with the other guys at the Butte Selective Service Center. He was so stoned on acid he didn't know what was going on. I was a hick farmboy who never owned more than one pair of shoes and who barely graduated from a high school with an eleven-member student body and a part-time teacher. The sergeant came out and said for everyone whose name he called to step forward across the white line on the floor. He read a bunch of names and everyone except Acid Freak and I were called across the line. The sergeant looked at the group, congratulated them on joining the new Action Army and marched them out of the room. At first, we thought we had lucked our way out of the draft. But then he turned to us and laughed. 'You, you poor SOBs,' he said, 'you guys are Marines!' The sergeant laughed every time he saw us."

Donnely's first assignment after boot camp wasn't that bad, considering he was a Marine. The Corps gave him a second pair of shoes and assigned him to a security detail for a Navy weather station on an island in the middle of the Pacific. Donnely, a sergeant and an officer. The three of them guarded about a million dollars' worth of thermometers in a climate where the temperature never varied. Originally a whole battalion was supposed to be on the island, but the Pentagon computer messed up and assigned only the three Marines. The officer and the sergeant spent so much time quarreling over how things were to be done that Donnely had the island and his time pretty much to himself.

There wasn't much to do on the island. The computer had equipped it fairly well before the error was discovered. The barracks and mess were adequate, even comfortable. There was lots of room. The two scientists on the island did all the cooking and cleaning, so Donnely was spared those chores. But there was nothing to do. There was no one to secure the island against. If there had been, those three Marines probably wouldn't have done much securing. There was no movie theater or television and only armed forces radio. None of the other four people on the island would play any of the recreational games with Donnely, so he had time pretty much on his hands. The first month he almost went crazy. Then he found the library.

The computer set up a library with over ten thousand books, everything from art to zoology. Donnely had read maybe ten books before coming to the island. But now he had two pairs of shoes and lots of time on his hands. During the second month he read a Hardy Boys mystery, *Tom Sawyer*, the Army textbook on American government for the high school graduation equivalency diploma and *Grimm's Fairy Tales*. The third month on the island he read eleven other books, the fourth month he read nineteen. By the sixth month he was reading at least a book a day, and by the eleventh month he was up to a minimum of two books a day. It took him two days each of almost straight reading to get through *The Brothers Karamazov*, *Don Quixote* and *War and Peace*. Donnely finagled a year extension of his assignment on the island by signing up for another year with the Corps. Fifteen months, three weeks and two days after he started reading, Donnely finished volume 9,999, *Webster's Second International Unabridged Dictionary*. The same day he got orders to rotate to Vietnam. Donnely stole volume 10,000 and took it with him. It was *The Complete Sherlock Holmes*.

I remember sitting around nights with Donnely and Frank Douglas, talking and drinking beer, occasionally doing other things, which if I admit to right now might make the governor take back his full pardon, so we won't go into any details except to say that a lot of people do it and as I write this it's still illegal everywhere but Nepal, where they are already so high they must figure a little higher won't hurt. Anyway, we would talk for *hours*. Donnely would tell us about all the things he had read in books and about how he was

11

trying to work out A Plan. He said he wanted to find A Plan which would take care of him and fix it so he would never be sent to another place like Vietnam or back to the harsh ranch in Montana. He said The Plan included me because I saved his life and had a special talent and Frank Douglas because he was trustworthy and a great friend. Frank and I thought he was a little goofy then, but we shouldn't have.

Frank, of course, talked a lot about his family. Frank also talked about dying. When he talked like that, Donnely and I would try to change the subject, but Frank kept insisting he knew he was going to get killed, so he had to plan things out.

Frank turned out to be right, but we didn't know that until after he was killed.

I mostly listened during those nights.

Except for Frank's death, the rest of our tour in Nam was uneventful. Donnely and I rotated back to the States together. I had a year left to go in my hitch, but he was through. When we said good-bye at the cab stand in San Diego, I figured I would never see the guy again. Just before he got in the taxi, Donnely looked at me and said, "Jack, I'll come for you. I don't know when yet but when The Plan is ready, I'll come get you. Keep loose until then and take care of yourself."

I said sure, slapped him on the back, watched the cab drive away and tried not to cry.

Donnely was a good man.

I got out of the Marines the next year, June 28, 1970, to be exact. I spent the next four years and some odd months bumming around. I tried college for a year, but while I did OK, I didn't like it. It was too much like the Marines with icing. I held about a dozen jobs over that period of time, working at them until I got bored, everything from heavy equipment operator to shoe salesman, which was what I was when Donnely found me on April 30, 1975. I was on my lunch break. Normally I took an hour, but we were having "Spring Madness Sale-a-thon," and the boss said I could only have thirty minutes. I was sitting in the McDonald's chewing my soggy Big Mac and thinking about ugly, smelly feet when this guy sits down across from me and says, "Hello, Jack."

12

It was Donnely all right. He looked pretty much the same, tall, thin, short sandy hair combed flat and cut in a longish crew cut. I think he even had on the same pair of jeans as when I sent him off into the wide world by himself that afternoon in San Diego.

We slapped each other on the back a few times, grinning and laughing. He asked me what I had been doing and I told him. I asked him the same and he was kind of vague, mentioning he tried college too and had done some other things.

Finally Donnely looked at me and asked, "Are you happy, Jack?"

I leaned back in my stool, dragging my tie through a catsup spill on the table. I always do things like that. I thought about all those ugly, smelly feet and screaming housewives waiting for me at the shoe store. I thought about what I would do that night, watch TV or have a couple of drinks in a couple of bars and literally kill a couple of hours. I looked at Donnely and said, "No, not really."

Then he goes and does something which almost made me mad. He grins. Me unhappy, and he grins! I'm halfway through thinking what an ungrateful SOB he is when he says, "Good, then I can help you. I've got The Plan."

Now this sends me back to Nam and those long nights' bull sessions. Donnely and The Plan. Frank and I once talked about Donnely and The Plan. At first we thought Donnely was just well read and a little strange from being such an isolated hick country boy. But we realized we had been wrong when we got to know him better. The Marine Corps had drafted an uninspired genius, then fed the genius' mind and given him two pairs of shoes. We knew that if Donnely ever hit on his plan, it would be a beaut, an almost guaranteed surefire success.

"Is it good?" I asked, one of my many stupid questions.

"It's excellent," he replied, his eyes glistening the way they did when Frank or I gave him a book he hadn't read. "But I need you and I want you, to say nothing of owing you."

I tried to wave that last remark aside, but he ignored me and continued.

13

"It will be risky, dangerous, exciting and challenging. In short, it will be full of things that will make it fun and worth doing. It will also be highly profitable. But I need you. Will you come?"

I looked at the remnants of my soggy Big Mac, then back to Donnely and his glistening blue eyes. "Yes," I said.

I had never seen him smile like that. He slapped me on the back and said, "Good. When can I expect you?"

About that time a huge fat lady sitting at the next table belched and picked up her third Big Mac. She took half of it in one bite, chewed twice and spoke to her fidgety skinny companion through a soggy mouthful of bun and burger: "I jus' can' wait until we ge' 'o th' sho' sale!"

I smiled at Donnely as I undid my tie and said, "Now."

Sometimes I blame the fat lady for throwing the pebble in the pond.

PHASE I

The Preliminaries

"Are you sure this is legal?"

Donnely put down the envelope he had been opening to look at me when he replied to my question. "Let's put it this way," he said. "The Professor and I both agree that it is not explicitly illegal. Therefore, logical extension seems to indicate that we are treading on thin but negotiable ice. Does that answer your question?"

It really didn't but I kept opening envelopes anyway. The dollar bills went to the pile on the left, the checks made out to cash went to the pile in the middle, the money orders or other easily negotiable currencies went to the pile on the right, and everything else (except stamps, which we put in a box provided by Alfred) joined the empty envelopes in the discard pile on the floor.

We were in Alfred's garage in Sacramento. We would have been in Alfred's house, but Alfred's house was so full of junk he had to move into the garage. We didn't want to disturb his junk piles even if there had been room, so we were in the garage too, opening envelopes and extracting money sent to us by the good and the guilty people of the great state of California, U.S.A.

One night those of us involved in The Plan—except Alfred and Donnely—tried to figure out Alfred's age. The guesses ran from eighteen to ninety-four. I figure one was as good as another, because with people like Alfred age doesn't matter. Besides The Group, nothing matters to or for Alfred except what he calls "his work." If that sounds a little crazy to you, you're right, because Alfred is a Mad Scientist.

Donnely said he found Alfred while working as a clerk in the Patent Office in Washington, D.C. Donnely said he thought the best way to find a Mad Scientist was to be in a place a Mad Scientist would be sure to come. (You might try to remember this principle of Donnely's. It will help you to understand some of what happens later.) So, in 1972, Donnely became a clerk in the Patent Office. It was all part of The Plan. Donnely met Alfred when the Mad Scientist came in to register his Gamathon Fertility Ray, a slightly modified version of his Gamathon Death Ray. I still don't know if Alfred has a patent for either of those inventions, but that's incidental and extraneous to this story. Donnely knew a lot about Alfred from reading the Patent Office's Special Inventors' Inventory Dossier or, as it is called in D.C., the Crackpot File. Alfred was Donnely's first choice for The Plan's Mad Scientist with the second option being an anemic grade school science teacher from Carbondale, Illinois, who claimed he was on the track of the perpetual-motion machine but things wouldn't slow down enough to let him find it. Alfred came to D.C. first, and Donnely, whom Reginald (you haven't met him yet) calls The Indomitable Donnely, persuaded Alfred to partake in The Plan.

This was long before I entered the operational stages of The Plan. Alfred was already "on board," as was Raoul (you'll meet him later, too). But I alone can claim I was in on the thing from the very start during those long Vietnamese nights.

When I met Alfred, I had a flash of doubt about my decision to join The Plan. Alfred looks like a skinny Albert Einstein, wispy white hair, always in need of a shave but never bearded, stoop-shouldered and jittery. When Donnely introduced him as the Mad Scientist, I could only say, "Of course."

Alfred seems to like his label. Reginald once said it was a pity Alfred wasn't born when Mad Scientist movies were being churned out by the carload. Hollywood would have made Alfred famous or vice versa.

One lady from San Luis Obispo enclosed a note with her

18

money. She said she hoped she hadn't caused us any trouble by being so late with her payment. I smiled as I threw her note on the discard pile and put her dollar bill on the money pile. She hadn't caused us any trouble.

Now you may wonder why otherwise insane Californians were calmly sending Donnely, Alfred and your humble narrator dollar bills and other similar monies. If you are wondering, it must be because you haven't seen the ad. The prosecution tried to introduce it as evidence of intent during the trial, but the judge, after listening to a string of counterarguments presented by the Professor (you'll meet him later, too), ruled the ad was irrelevant and inadmissible, to say nothing of unneeded. *Time* magazine, however, did do a nice job of reprinting it in the second cover story they did on us. The ad looks like this:

NOTICE:
TO ALL CALIFORNIA TAXPAYERS

All duly registered private taxpayers of the State of California have until the end of the month to pay their $1 (one dollar) registration fee. This year no late fees will be accepted and failure to pay the fee may result in action. Fee payments should be mailed to Treasurer, P.O. Box 6973, Sacramento, California.

The ad ran in twenty-five California newspapers for three days, starting the fifteenth of June. We received more than fifteen hundred pounds of mail, including $74,361.25 in cash or easily negotiable paper and God knows how much in discarded checks, all from dutious citizens or warily guilty taxpayers.

The beauty of Donnely's scheme was that it is not illegal. The ads were bought and paid for. Nowhere in the ad did we purport to be a government agency entitled to solicit or receive funds. Nor did we threaten or coerce. An "action" can be almost anything. We merely asked for money, and money we got.

19

Of course, Donnely knew it was such a good thing it couldn't last. He also knew somebody in authority was bound to question the whole matter. But he and the Professor agreed it was worth the time and effort, as indeed it was.

It was July 1. Donnely decided today would be the last day we would pick up the mail until he was ready for another stage of the operation. I had no idea what that stage was, but since the first stage went so well and so profitably, I didn't argue. Besides, Donnely told me I had an important errand to run with him.

I've often wondered if his timing on this was the result of luck or something else.

As we drove to the airport (Donnely drove, I rode), I congratulated Donnely on The Plan. After expenses, he, Alfred, the Professor and myself stood to clear approximately eighteen thousand dollars apiece. (I hadn't met Raoul yet then either.) The Plan was profitable.

Donnely glanced sideways at me as we pulled into the airport parking lot. "Surely," he said almost reproachfully, "you don't think this little operation is The Plan? A measly, small financial gain, The Plan?"

"Well," I asked somewhat puzzledly, "if this isn't The Plan, what is it?"

"A mere preliminary," he replied as he whipped Alfred's old red pickup truck into a parking spot near the terminal. "A mere preliminary." As we walked through the glass doors and into the crowded terminal, he dropped the bomb on me: "We're going to rob a bank."

I'm still not sure how I made it to the departure-arrival area, how I kept my composure. Donnely planned to rob a bank, a bank with vaults, guards, guns and bullets and me. And me! All sorts of visions—prison, money, machine-gunning guards, steel bars, Sunday visits when no one came, mail call, evil villains in showers—erupted in my mind. By the time I regained my composure we were standing by an American Airlines arrival gate and the loudspeaker was blaring about the arrival of New York to Sacramento Flight 409, now unloading. I wanted to blare

20

back, to yell to the world and to Donnely. "No!" I would yell. "Not me! I won't rob any bank with you! I won't get shot up! I won't go to prison!"

Now let me say here, so I can save you the trouble of calling me hypocritical in a few pages, I have no compunction about robbing banks. I don't like banks. Banks remind me of big, hulking sponges, squatting on main streets and soaking up a little from everything that goes by them. Banks are a meretricious (I learned that word in prison) cross between a whirlpool and a mugger. I wouldn't mind getting a little comfort from a bank, if I could figure out some way to do it free. But banks don't work that way. Either they take your money and you are satisfied with what they give you or you don't have anything to do with them. You most definitely do not try to take their money. They kill people for things like that. I don't want to die.

So I was ready to tell Donnely thanks but no thanks, it's been fun, swell, a lot of laughs, but see you around if you need a pair of shoes to run from the cops in, when Meredith Douglas walked coolly out of the disembarking airplane and into The Plan and my life.

Of course, I didn't know it was Meredith Douglas then. Introductions came later. I did know it was an angel sent from heaven, probably not for me. Her long, cool legs quickly shortened the distance between us, her slender but rounded hips swaying slightly below her thin waist, her shoulders firmly squared and supporting both her easily sufficient bosom and her beautiful face. Her naturally straight black hair was cut short into what they call a modified pageboy, and two huge brown eyes watched the world with the kind of easy, unassuming confidence perfection brings. Her ebony skin shone.

I watched her with that sinking feeling, which would come when she passed me by, already building in my stomach. I sank even more when she smiled and stopped right in front of me and said, "You must be Jack Mason. I'm Meredith Douglas and I've waited so long to meet you!"

The thousand and one things I could have said left my

mind and I could only stare. Such bliss couldn't be true! Before the pause could turn into a mutually awkward situation, Donnely inserted his lanky frame between us. "I'm Donnely," he said, which, of course, was all he had to say.

I moved to where I could once again watch Meredith's lovely face. I saw her eyes light up at the sound of Donnely's name and heard her say, "Oh, Mr. Donnely! I'm so happy to meet you!"

Whomp!

My heart, which only seconds before had been catapulted to the sky off a trampoline, fell back to the gym floor without the comfort of safety mats.

Donnely smiled back and said, "You don't look at all like Frank."

Then it hit me. Meredith Douglas. She was Frank Douglas' little sister.

The three of us turned to walk to the truck. I bent down and picked up two heavy strange-looking suitcases Meredith had set down when she saw us. She flashed me a dazzling smile and my heart once again began to flutter. Donnely squashed it with his combat boot (the second pair of shoes given him by the Marines). His strong arms easily relieved me of my burden after they deposited some slips of paper in my shirt pocket. "Here," he said, "pick up her other bags at the check station and meet us at the truck."

I watched them walk away, my leader and my lovely. I felt like throwing up. Instead, I trotted off and fetched the bags like a good little boy.

Meredith's other bags were definitely not filled with gossamer wings. More likely lead weights. I tried to fight gravity, the pushing crowd and perspiration-caused odor as I lugged them back to the truck. I also tried to fight insanity. I know I lost the first three battles and I'm not sure about the fourth. Thoughts of Meredith, bank robbery, dead Frank Douglas and Donnely kept destroying my rational process. I was still confused when I reached the truck.

Meredith sat in the passenger seat. "Where's Donnely?" I asked.

Her voice was softly cool. "He had to rent a car. He said we were to meet him at this address right away."

Her fingertips brushed mine as she handed me a slip of paper. My hand shook and I almost dropped the address.

I have no idea how many people I terrified with my driving that afternoon. To say the least, my mind wasn't on the road. I remember an inordinately large number of horn blasts, angry shouts and at least one terrified scream. I remember weaving back and forth across seemingly unimportant white lines. I remember some rather trying corners, but I don't remember much else about the traffic or my driving. I do remember I didn't scare Meredith and I remember everything she said.

Ever try to watch someone and hang on her every word while driving down an expressway during noon rush hour? I'll let your imagination take over and just describe our dialogue. I started out with one of my usual witty, perceptive, intelligent, charming, worldly comments.

"So you're Frank Douglas' sister."

Pretty good, huh? Really suave. She replied, "Yes," and we were off and running.

"I remember Frank talking about you." I did, but I had thought of her as a skinny, awkward pubescent.

"He wrote me a lot about you, too. I mean, Mr. Donnely and you." My heart sank. "He said you and Donnely were the best men in the world, his best friends. He said if I could ever do anything to help either of you, I should. He also told me that if he didn't make it back from Vietnam"—she swallowed here and I once again cursed the company intelligence officer— "I was to take his place in The Plan."

That part of the ride I do remember. I almost wiped out a bakery truck. "You mean you know about The Plan?"

She shrugged and I almost fainted as the front of her blouse moved. "I know Donnely is a wonderful man and a genius. I know he has a plan Frank was involved in, a plan Frank said would take care of us. And I know Donnely wants me in The Plan like he wanted Frank, so here I am."

"But you don't know anything about The Plan?"

23

She smiled and my foot pressed the accelerator to the floor. "No," she replied. "I suppose I'm stupid trusting Donnely like I do, but he seems like such a special person and he's so competent, so confident, so nice. And Frank says he's a genius. So I trust him. No matter what he says to do, I'll do it. Are you in The Plan, too?"

I thought about that one for a long time. It was the one time during the ride that my eyes didn't keep darting to look at Meredith. Of course, I could still smell her soft warm loveliness, but at least I didn't look at her. I thought about Donnely's bank-robbing statement. I thought about guards, guns, bullets and prison. Then I thought about Meredith.

"Yes," I said slowly, "I'm part of The Plan."

I can't really bring myself to blame Meredith for anything, so she must not have been the one who threw the pebble in the pond.

During the rest of the ride I learned about her background. After Frank died, she quit college and left their home in Seattle for New York. She worked for a while as a model, but, she said in a half-complaining tone, she was too "developed" to fit the standard model image.

Every time I thought of her development I wove over the median line.

She gave up her career as a model but stayed in the profession, working her way up from makeup girl and darkroom assistant to an assistant photographer. She gave up a chance to take over the head photographer's position at a high-paying fashion magazine, all because she had faith in her brother and he had faith in Donnely and Donnely had The Plan.

I ask you, what could I do? She put all her lovely eggs in Donnely's basket. Could I but do the same, hopefully right next to her eggs?

We beat Donnely to the address, a dilapidated house in one of the fringe poverty neighborhoods. I felt right at home. Meredith looked like an Egyptian queen touring the slave quarters.

It was a strange house. Upstairs there were two bedrooms,

24

small, almost closets. Downstairs there were the living room, the kitchen and a hall-reception room. The only furniture in the whole place was a desk and three chairs in the living room. There were also four rather peculiar floor lights facing the desk from each of its corners. I turned one on. The glare was terrific. It lit up part of the desk as if darkness had been there before instead of the half-light coming from the dusty windows. It reminded me of a Gestapo interrogation light. I switched it off.

The next thing I noticed was the mountain of paper on the floor by the desk. It looked familiar, so I picked up some of it. Empty envelopes, all addressed to the Treasurer at our Post Office Box. So that was what Donnely had done with all the empty envelopes. But why had he brought them here?

I looked at the four blank walls, then up the ceiling. Just above the desk, slightly to its left side, was a hole about three inches in diameter. I called Meredith's attention to it just as Donnely entered.

We exchanged greetings. I noticed Meredith greeted him quite warmly. That didn't make me feel any better. Donnely glanced quickly around the room.

"Everything looks OK. Jack, move the pickup up the street a couple of blocks and lock it up tight. Then come back here. We've got an errand to run. Meredith, I'm sorry to put you to work right away—"

"Oh, no, that's quite all right." Her eager voice cut his apology short.

I slunk from the room as he was telling her, "Good. Now bring your equipment and come with me. I think you'll find. . . ."

Donnely met me at the front door when I got back. As we drove away in the car (Donnely behind the wheel), I watched the windows of the old house. She didn't wave.

We went to the post office. Box 6973 didn't contain the usual notice telling us to call for our sacks of mail at the window. Instead, there were only three letters. I thought this was strange, but Donnely smiled and said it was according to plan.

As we drove back to the house (I was once again a passenger), I noticed he kept glancing in the rearview mirror and smiling. Once he stopped the car in an intersection and backed up because the light turned orange. I thought this was silly, because he would have had plenty of time to make it across, but I said nothing. I was too blue.

When we pulled up to the curb, he glanced at a car parking about a block down the street behind us.

"Quick," he said, "we've got to be ready."

I had to jog to follow him closely. He left the door unlocked.

"Are you ready, Meredith?" His voice boomed as he ran behind the desk, pausing only to switch on all four lights. Meredith yelled from upstairs that all was in readiness. I followed Donnely's wave to sit in one of the chairs.

When they knocked on the door, Donnely broke into a smile. He began to open an envelope, carefully keeping the desk clear of paper pieces. "Let the gentlemen in," he said.

There were four of them. Ever notice how federal officials, cops or not, always seem to travel in pairs and pairs of pairs? Like shoes? At least, that's one of the things I noticed during the whole affair.

The tallest one was only five eight. He flashed me a set of credentials, said, "FBI," and strode right by me.

"Who the hell is it?" Donnely's voice boomed from inside the room.

Two of the other men brushed by me. The third encouraged me to join them by using a wrist lock I had seen in basic. It's called a come-along and that's what I did.

The tall one strode to the desk. He stopped outside the glare of the lights and started his speech. "I am an agent of the Federal Bureau of Investigation and I have here—"

"Now hold everything one minute," demanded Donnely in his most impressive commanding voice. Donnely could freeze a charging bull with that voice. Needless to say, the FBI agent shut up.

Donnely continued. "Now you may be an FBI agent and then again you may not. Give me your identification." Donnely reached out his hand.

26

There was a moment's hesitation on the agent's part; then Donnely snapped his fingers. I closed my eyes, waiting for the G-man to pull his gun and blast the impudent punk. When I opened them, Donnely was putting the FBI agent's folder flat on the desk, face up. Donnely studied it from that angle for several seconds; then for some strange reason he turned it the other way around and studied the plastic genuine imitation leather back. Finally he handed it back to the agent and said, "Now before we all waste a lot of time, let me ask if any of you is an attorney."

The smallest man in the group identified himself as an attorney from the California attorney general's office, criminal prosecution bureau. When he said that, I swallowed my confidence and sent a prayer that they wouldn't find Meredith upstairs. I glanced heavenward and my eyes fell on the hole in the ceiling. Or rather, what used to be the hole in the ceiling, for now it was filled with what looked like glass. I quickly glanced back at the desk.

The attorney general's man's words didn't seem to faze Donnely at all. He merely replied, "Good," and launched into a technical legal discussion of which I understood very little and remember nothing. He and the Professor had spent hours working that one out. Donnely ended with: "so legally all you can do is issue a temporary restraining order prohibiting us from engaging in subsequent solicitation until you as the state have time to make an adequate disclaimer of our possible connection with you. To save you gentlemen that trouble, I have mailed a signed, sworn statement to the attorney general saying that as of July 1, I shall desist from this activity. Now since you gentlemen have no further legal business here, I suggest you leave."

And, after a short huddled conference, they did.

I waited until I heard their car drive away before I exhaled.

Donnely called Meredith downstairs and gave us our instructions. He and I would drive away immediately, checking for tails and losing them. After we left the rented car off downtown, we would call Meredith. If we hadn't been tailed, it was probable the house wasn't being watched and

27

she could drive the truck downtown to meet us. If we were tailed, the house was probably being watched. Donnely said he had an alternative plan to get her out after dark in that event.

We didn't need Donnely's alternative plan because we weren't tailed. Either the FBI was slipping or they decided we weren't worth the trouble.

I spent the ride (Donnely drove) downtown thinking. While we sat in the park waiting for Meredith to pick us up, I talked to Donnely about my ideas.

"Let me ask you something," I said. "You knew all along we were going to be questioned by the FBI, didn't you?"

Donnely smiled. He saw I was analyzing what was going on. He always says my biggest flaw is I often just accept things as I think they seem instead of analyzing them as they are. "Yes," he replied, "I did, or at least I greatly expected they would. The probability was extremely high."

I thought I saw the light, or at least part of it. "So that's why you rented the house and made it look like we were operating there, right? So the FBI couldn't find out we are really working out of Alfred's, right?"

"Well," he said, "partially. Tell me, Jack, did you notice the hole in the ceiling above the desk?"

Now that made me angry. Donnely also tells me that sometimes I'm not observant enough. I remember thinking at the time that it was strange that I was suddenly bothered by Donnely's criticisms. I never had been before. "Of course I noticed," I said. "I even noticed that there was glass in it when—"

Now I'm dumb and not too analytical and sometimes not very observant, but when you hit me with a sledgehammer, I notice.

"Pictures!" I yelled. "You took pictures of their identification! That's what Meredith was doing upstairs, that's why the hole was in the ceiling, that's why the lights!"

Donnely was grinning and nodding.

"Wait a minute," I said, "wait a minute. Don't tell me . . . please don't tell me we went through this whole thing with the money in the mail just so you could get some pictures of FBI IDs!"

"Oh, no," he said casually, "that was only half the reason."

I swallowed, not really wanting to ask the next question. I did anyway. "What is the other half of the reason for the mail solicitation thing?"

I think he was genuinely surprised. "Why, to get money, of course."

Try for an extra point, I thought. "What for?"

"To finance the bank robbery."

Just then Meredith drove up and tooted the truck horn. Donnely waved and walked gaily toward the truck. I followed slowly.

To finance the bank robbery. Of course.

The Plan

We shifted our base of operations, as the military would
say, from Sacramento to Los Angeles, a switch I didn't
particularly relish. I was beginning to find out just how
complicated The Plan was, a discovery which both
encouraged and baffled me. For instance, we each had a Los
Angeles apartment in a large building and each of our
buildings was within a two-block radius of the apartment
which served as headquarters. Nobody lived at headquarters,
but all of us spent a lot of time there. The neighborhood was
one of those young singles areas, the neighborhoods in
which the elderly people are pushing thirty-five and the cars
in the parking lots still have high school graduation tassels
dangling from the rearview mirrors. Since this was Los
Angeles, with Hollywood only a squeal on the freeway away,
we were surrounded by the Beautiful People who while away
the hours before cinema directors discover them by sunning
along the pools and drawing unemployment. I have never
seen so many beautiful tanned blondes in my life.

I guess I should have enjoyed myself more during our stay
in Los Angeles. Even the most ardent movie oglers among
the blond bodies liked a change of pace, and a nonfuture star
like me could have really made hay, as they say. In fact,
Raoul did (make hay). But after a week of exploding
exposure, all the blondes tended to look and sound alike.
Besides, Meredith was there.

Officially, I had been renting my apartment for three
months before I even saw it. That goes to show you how
organized Donnely was. He had Raoul rent places for all of

us long before we became "operational," as they say in the government.

My place was OK, furnished, a small living room, kitchen-dining area, bedroom and a bathroom mercifully equipped with a shower-tub combination. It was a much better place than the one I was living in when Donnely found me. Raoul certainly had excellent luck in apartment hunting, but then he was good at whatever Donnely told him to do.

That was partially because Raoul O'Connor is in his own way a genius, much as is Donnely. Since you haven't met Raoul yet, I'd better introduce him to you.

Raoul's mother met his father at confession. Of course, Raoul's father wasn't a a Father, or he wouldn't have met Raoul's mother and become a father. Those were the days when once a Father, *always* a Father. Anyway, Raoul's future father was not a Father; he was a sneak thief preying on the purses of ladies while they were in the confessional. Raoul's mother caught him, but rather than turn him in, she decided to marry and reform the Irish rogue and turn him into a good Puerto Rican husband. Raoul's father considered the consequences of being caught with his crime and he considered the supple form of Raoul's mother. It was an easy choice. The church Father was overjoyed that two of his parishioners had met and fallen in love in the cathedral. They were married that same week.

If you want to know what Raoul looks like, drive by the neighborhood pool hall, the hamburger haven hangout or any other similar cultural gathering point for the society of young punks. They all look the same, slouching against walls, leaning "comfortably" in impossible positions, wearing uniforms which vary with the season and the city, but all basically look the same. Their faces have a kind of ruthless dullness about them and their eyes seem to follow you wherever you go, like the Mona Lisa. Americans used to call them greasers, the English call them rockers or teddy boys, and they call themselves cool.

Raoul looks almost exactly like all the others except for two things, his eyes and his mouth. He is short and muscularly

31

stocky, his black hair looks greasy even right after he has washed it, he has pimple scars on his lean, hawkish face, and his blue jeans and rumpled T-shirt always look slightly worn and dirty despite the fact that Raoul is immaculate. He wears shiny black combat boots or tennis shoes, all depending on his mood. Donnely made sure Raoul had two pairs of shoes. The two physical things which set Raoul apart from the rest of the punks are his eyes and his mouth. His eyes sparkle and seem to have life behind them. Punks' eyes are almost always dull, vacant. When they have anything behind them, it usually seems ugly. Raoul's mouth is always slightly curved in a smile, a genuinely amused smile. Punks' mouths usually droop dully; even their grins droop.

Donnely says these two differences showed him Raoul probably had two of the five assets he was looking for in a future Group member. Donnely says the smile shows a knowledgeable sense of humor and the eyes show alert intelligence. Donnely said the necessary probability for success factors would have been satisfied with two out of five of the assets present, and we lucked out with Raoul because he also possessed the other three assets, toughness, loyalty and individuality, plus a genius-level knack for improvisation.

Donnely found Raoul by engaging in a certain type of commercial activity in which he would meet a lot of young people, at least some of whom would possess the qualities he needed in an individual to recruit for The Plan. That was in 1972, so you can see how long Donnely had been building the operation. The commercial activity provided Donnely with a considerable cash profit for his operating expenses as well as helped him find Raoul. See how cleverly Donnely works things! He always says one should make the most out of everything and he does.

Meredith, Donnely and I flew to Los Angeles, Alfred drove over in his old red pickup truck, bringing several boxes of equipment. I still don't know what all he brought, but it's not really necessary. Raoul met us at the airport, grinning and waving as we stepped off the plane.

32

It was hard to hear introductions, mainly because of Raoul's transistor radio. He takes that radio with him everywhere he goes. The jets taking off and landing didn't help any. The conversation went something like this:

"*. . . . and that, all you wonderful brothers and sisters out there cruisin' or losin', makes no difference to your old Fat Dad, he loves you just the same, was Franky Vallee and the Four Seasons coming out of the Backroom of Yesterday* (echoing voice in the background: '*Yesterday . . . Yesterday . . . Yesterday . . .* ') *carrying with them that Oldy Goldy Goody But Goney 'Rag Doll.' Now for all you cats out Hawthorne way, beautiful suburb of downtown LA* (echoing voice in the background: '*The Big One . . . One . . . One . . .* ') *here's another Memory Maker from KUUL* (booming bass voice in the background: '*Radio Coooooool!*') *brought to you by your own Fat Dad and. . . .*"

"Meredith, Jack, I'd like you to meet. . . ."

VAROOMMMNNNNNNNNRRRSHSHSHSHOOOSH!

". . . 'ul O'Connor. Raoul, this is. . . ."

"*. . . Phred and the Phantoms! Our own rocking rangers riding their big machine from yesterday (. . . Yesterday . . . Yesterday . . . Yesterday . . .) with a very special chick. Dig it! (. . . Dig it! . . . Dig it! . . . Dig it! . . .)* Music:
          "Someone ran my heart away,"

". . . just call me Raoul, OK?"

"Right, Raoul *(my voice)*. Say, do you suppose you could turn the radio. . . ."

VAROOMMMNNNNNNNNRRRSHSHSHSHOOSH!

"What did you say? I couldn't hear you over those damn jets!"

"I said. . . ."

> *"So now you gotta. . . .*
> *run wi' me, Shirley!*
> *Run my love a better way!"*

Get the picture? Actually, it isn't too bad talking to Raoul if you aren't around an airport or any jackhammers. After a while you get so used to the radio racket it kind of fades into the background.

33

Raoul and I got along very well, once I decided he wasn't interested in Meredith. Not that Raoul didn't like girls, not that by any means. The only trouble we had with him was on account of girls. Sometimes he would show up a little late for meetings and so exhausted he couldn't even turn up the radio when one of his many favorite songs came on. He damn near died from sexual indulgence, but he built a legend for himself with the blond starlets that lasted at least a record six months after he left.

I once asked Raoul if he didn't think he should slow down a little. He looked at me and said with a wise voice not befitting his twenty-one years or delinquent appearance, "Jack, my motto is that to truly appreciate satisfying moderation, one must first overindulge. You might say my conscience demands I try my best to live up to that philosophy."

Actually, what could I say?

I suppose while we're making introductions you should meet the rest of The Group, all of them except the Professor, that is. I'll save him for later, when the introduction will mean more. You've already met Donnely, Meredith, Alfred, Raoul and, of course, me. There are two more members of The Group, as we like to call ourselves, besides the Professor: Reginald Worthington and Larry Cordingley. A grand total of eight "operatives," as the Washington *Post* called us.

In a way I wish there were less of us. A couple of the others feel that way, too. Not that we would want to lose any member of The Group or that The Plan could afford that, but it is just the number, eight. One less and we could be The Magnificent Seven. Reginald especially likes this idea, since he is somewhat superstitious and seven is historically a lucky number. But there are eight of us, which explains why we call ourselves The Group. You can't really make a snappy title using the mumber eight.

Back to the introductions. Reginald Worthington is one of Hollywood's truly great actors, only most people don't know that. Most movie fans don't even realize that they have seen Reginald in literally hundreds of pictures. I'll name three of his favorite roles for you: He played a policeman in *Brewster*

McCloud, a wounded soldier in *M*A*S*H* and a Roman centurion accompanying Richard Burton in *Antony and Cleopatra*. Reginald regrets that he didn't get to accompany Richard Burton everywhere, but such is life when you're a famous crowd scene and character actor.

Reginald is blessed with a physical ability any true actor would sell his soul to possess. Something about Reginald allows him literally to assume the role he is cast for, and assume it in such a way that his own physical characteristics and mannerisms disapppear, leaving only the pure character. He was the cop's cop, the most damaged of the wounded, an emperor's centurion. However, in this day of famous actors appearing as characters, with the emphasis on the person doing the acting and not the character being portrayed, Reginald cannot be a star. Look at it this way: How could a woman have a crush on Robert Redford (and therefore go to all his movies) if she was never sure what he looked like, if one minute in one picture he looked like a spy named Condor and the next minute in another picture he looked like someone else? Understand? That's why Reginald is not a star.

When Reginald is being Reginald, which is seldom because he actually relishes his chameleon ability (we called him Chameleon for a code name) and is always slipping in and out of roles, he looks quite normal, almost nondescript. So I won't ruin his later characters by describing him now, except to say Reginald as himself looks like your average middle-aged Caucasian male.

Donnely found Chameleon by running an ad in *Daily Variety* for an established male character actor with a good deal of picture experience, some theater work and no public recognition. Reginald was the third and last person he interviewed. Donnely knows how to spot talent.

Donnely convinced Reginald to join The Plan partially by promising him tremendous financial gain. But we all knew Reginald's real motivation was that The Plan allowed him to play a starring role full time, in front of a demanding audience. The tantalizing challenge was too much to resist.

For a while I couldn't understand why we had the eighth

member of the team at all. I mean, we had Alfred, so why did we need another technician? Now you may think Alfred is a kook, but he's not, he's a Mad Scientist. Sure, he makes screwy things like a Gravitation Occultator, but that doesn't mean he's not a first-class scientist. Mad though he may be, Alfred can whip things up in a lab like you wouldn't believe. He can also do the old standard tricks, like electrolysis of water and chemical analysis. So if we had Alfred, why did we need Larry Cordingley?

Donnely explained it to me. Larry's expertise was mechanical. He could fix this or that, cross-wire circuits until they practically produced their own electricity, tune engines suitable for Grand Prix racing and pick locks almost as good as Raoul. Alfred, on the other hand, was good with technical things but only good, whereas Larry was an absolute flop at from-nothingness-to-completion original invention. Larry is unsurpassed at improvising and developing, once given the basic ideas and concepts, and Alfred is unsurpassed at providing basic ideas and concepts to develop. That subtle but important difference, said Donnely, made them both equally important to The Plan.

Donnely found Larry by sabotaging the phone systems in eleven major cities, so if you had trouble making calls in January, 1973, Donnely might be to blame instead of the phone company. It took Donnely eleven tries before he found a city phone company with a man good enough to unsabotage the phone system as easily as Donnely had sabotaged it. I want to tell you how you too can wreak havoc on the phone company, but the Professor says our pardon and our positions do not make us immune from future civil suits or conspiracy to commit vandalism charges, so I'll have to restrain myself. Donnely found Larry in Cincinnati, one of my favorite cities. It is lucky for the country that Cincinnati was high on Donnely's list of cities to be searched, or who knows how many people would have suddenly found their phones doing odd things like connecting them to prerecorded obscene phone callers? I always say the Cincinnati phone company gave the country a great gift by

36

having the foresight to employ Larry Cordingley so Donnely could find him and take him away with promises of profitable excitement through The Plan.

In a way, you might say the personnel manager of the Cincinnati phone company is a thrower of rocks into ponds.

Larry is only a little strange. He and Donnely are the workhorses of The Group. Larry is a mumbler, the kind of person who walks around muttering to himself. He is slightly under six feet tall, medium build with a tight, wiry frame. He's going bald, but it doesn't bother him. He always thinks everything is going to go wrong, but it never does, partially because he works so hard at making sure it doesn't. At first it looked as if he and Alfred might be jealous of each other, but within a few days of Larry flying into Los Angeles they were as thick as thieves.

Which, of course, they should have been since they were going to rob a bank.

Wally Kearns (you'll meet him later) once asked me if I had any trouble controlling the members of The Group. I evaded that question. I am afraid to go into details about anything with Wally, perhaps without reason, but certainly not without rationality, so I just mumbled something indefinite and changed the subject. Of course, Wally also asked the wrong question since nobody tries to control anybody else in The Group. I could have told him a large number of incidents which kept me hopping in the early phases of The Plan. Any time you mix a large number (say one or more) of geniuses together and try to organize them, you are bound to have problems. Our group had its share. Most of the problems came from trying to keep The Group together functioning as a group and unobtrusive while not forcing members to sacrifice too much of their "personal lifestyles," as *Rolling Stone* called them.

I've already mentioned we had trouble keeping Raoul off girls and vice versa. I think Donnely had some problems with the Professor, but he handled them so that none of us ever knew about them. I also think he may have had some problems with Meredith, but I avoided her to keep from coming apart at the seams. Donnely made me his sergeant-assistant and in that capacity I had to watch out for Alfred the Mad Scientist, Larry the Mechanical Marvel, Reginald the Dramatist, Raoul the Lover and, of course, myself. Let's take them in that order.

Alfred's life was "his work" and his work was a problem unto itself. In addition to all the materials he brought to help with The Plan, he shipped most of his equipment to LA so he could continue inventing. He rented a vacant garage behind one of the massive high-rise dormitory apartments and set up a lab. One night, while on the trail of the nerve gas we later used, our Afred followed in some of the footsteps of a Swedish Alfred (last name, Nobel) and rediscovered dynamite. The startling discovery blew our Alfred through the garage door (giving him only minor bruises and a stunned frustration) and burned the garage to the ground. The only way I was able to avoid an extensive and potentially dangerous police inquiry into the affair was to have Reginald play a Hollywood director (a role he disliked but had no trouble with) and have Raoul produce a stable of stunning, hopeful starlets to meet the police investigating team. They took one look at the bleached beauties and the obvious Hollywood director, deduced movie publicity stunt and disgustedly drove away without asking any questions.

Unlike Alfred, Larry posed problems that weren't directly related to his genius. They were more basic. Larry was a junkie. Not your average, run-of-the-mill heroin or booze or cigarette junkie, nothing routine like that. Larry was addicted to Red Cross sandwiches; unrecognizable, unidentifiable goo spread thinly between two slightly stale pieces of white bread and served by smiling female volunteers who can only be described as ladies. The only place you can get Red Cross sandwiches is at a Red Cross-sponsored event. Besides refugee camps and tedious volunteer meetings, the only common events the Red Cross sponsors and serves sandwiches at are disasters and blood drawings. Unfortunately for Larry, disasters seemed to avoid him. Unfortunately for The Group and me as the main

38

shepherd, blood drawings are fairly common. Larry had four separate blood drawing ID cards so he wo ıldn't have to wait the full eight weeks between donations and sandwich orgies. He has a hard time holding out. Larry's addiction posed a problem because when he was low on blood, his efficiency naturally dropped considerably. A sluggish mechanical genius is almost worse than no mechanical genius at all.

Donnely and I both tried on a number of occasions to convince him he should kick the habit. We tried making sandwiches for him, using a recipe supplied by a bribed Red Cross nurse (we bribed her with Raoul), but they just weren't the same. Part of it was the atmosphere, or so Reginald claims. We tried wearing white armbands with red crosses when we fed him, but that didn't help either. Using Donnely's argument of short-term deprivation to acquire long-term gain, I was able to convince Larry to moderate his need. I convinced him he could talk the Red Cross blood drawers into accepting large lumps of money instead of small amounts of his blood in trade for the sandwiches and that the bank job would give him that money. He reluctantly agreed to cut back to acceptable donation intervals until after the bank job.

But my experience in the Marines and Raoul's experience in the streets made us wary of Larry. Never trust junkies completely because sometimes they just can't help themselves. We checked Larry's arm for needle tracks at least once a day.

Like Alfred, Reginald presented a common problem manifested in a different way. Reginald constantly works at perfecting his technique. One of his ways of practicing his already polished skill is to hang around street corners, pick out interesting people and assume their identities. He can walk into a crowd as a bored commuter, switch to a stoned acid freak, convert to a vacationing Baptist minister and emerge as a corporate lawyer. While this ability usually gets him out of any trouble it gets him into, every once in a while his audience has no artistic taste or theatrical presence and

39

Reginald runs smack into a merciless critic. Then he needs help.

This happened once while I was shepherding him. He was "cruising" down the Sunset Strip, shifting characters regularly, when he crossed a streak of bad luck. He had just shifted from an IBM executive to a blossomed closet queen when he accidentally stepped on the toes of a repressed, vindictive vice cop. Reginald's astute character analysis immediately identified the cop for what he was, but before the actor could retreat and become someone else, a strong hand firmly grasped his wrist, which, in keeping with falsely stereotyped character, had been limply dangling. Reginald said he considered using a trick Raoul taught us to throw the cop but decided that might be bad politics. He was lucky he made that decision, for a uniformed motorcycle bull quickly came up behind him. So did I.

I had been looking for Reginald for an hour. Unfortunately I was a few minutes and a few characters too late. I knew I had to act fast, so I plowed my way past the two policemen, grabbed Reginald by the collar and said, "So there you are, Mr. Perkins. Naughty, naughty, naughty. The doctor will be very angry with you for walking away from the rest of the group. Come along now."

Reginald picked up on cue like a trouper, as they say on Broadway. He immediately assumed the contrite look of an escaped mental patient collared by an attendant. Because his performance was so excellent, he made my impersonation of the attendant seem believable. He also helped the cops cast themselves. The officers of the law even offered to help me escort my prisoner back to the sanitorium. I had a hard time turning their offer down.

The incident shows that while working with geniuses is trying and dangerous, their abilities usually come in handy.

That leaves Raoul and the shepherd himself and their problems. I've already explained Raoul and the troubles we had with him. I made it a practice to knock on every door behind which I heard rock music coming from a radio, just in case our Latin-Gaelic lover was exhausting himself inside.

You meet a lot of strange people that way. As for my problems, between feeling blue for Meredith, trying to keep my sanity and looking after the others, I didn't have time to have any.

Back to The Plan. For three weeks we met in the apartment headquarters, spending almost twelve hours a day getting to know one another and cross-training each other. Donnely wanted us to be able to tell exactly how and what the other Group members were thinking so we could act as a team with as little friction as possible. We did a lot of different things. Meredith taught us how to take pictures with all her various cameras and she taught Larry how to develop and print the photographs. I was a little miffed that I didn't get to spend those hours in the darkroom with her, but I wasn't jealous because Larry told me he didn't really find women as such all that interesting. He did, however, admire Meredith for her technical skills. She knows a lot about chemistry and art.

Meredith and Reginald spent a lot of time teaching us about makeup and Reginald taught us to act. I'll never forget the night Alfred delivered Mark Antony's funeral oration for Julius Caesar and Hamlet's "To be or not to be" soliloquy back to back. He was fantastic.

Alfred, Larry and Raoul taught us mechanics, everything from lock picking to hot-wiring a car. Raoul also taught us things like pickpocketing and self-defense. He had been captain of his high school's karate team as well as war lord of his neighborhood street gang. He showed me things my Marine drill instructors never heard of.

Donnely and I were the only members of The Group who didn't train the others. Of course, with Donnely this was understandable. He gave us almost daily lectures on everything from the right state of mind to team unity and perseverance. But I felt a little awkward, left out. Oh, sure, I got to read a long, rambling lecture by the Professor which explained legal tactics to use in case of trouble, but other than that I didn't seem to have much to contribute to The Group.

I brought that up one day when I was talking to Donnely. I asked him if, since I wasn't an expert or a genius, the only reason I was a member of The Group was his promise to do something for me because I saved his life. Was I merely a fetch-and-carry lump of dead weight?

He smiled at me and said, "Jack, do you think I would lie to you?"

I thought about that. Besides being a genius, Donnely was one thing for sure, honest. He lied to me only once, and then he had no choice, but that came much later. "No," I replied then, "you wouldn't lie to me."

"And you still don't know what your expertise is?" It wasn't said as if he were really asking a question.

"No," I replied again.

"Good. Because right now I think it would be bad for you to know what it is. I'll tell you when the proper time comes, but meantime, just believe me when I tell you that you are as much an expert as the Professor or Alfred or myself or any of us."

Now that made me do a lot of thinking, but it was all wasted effort. I had no idea what he meant.

Another conversation made me do a lot of thinking, too; only those thoughts were painful. I was talking to Larry one day during a break in our training. We were sitting in the window box watching the rest of The Group drink coffee at the kitchen table. At least he was watching The Group. I was watching Meredith.

Larry must have noticed my gaze because he said, "Yup, she sure is something."

Now I had been very careful not to show that I had lost my head over Meredith. I even went so far as to avoid her whenever I could bring myself to do it. I looked quickly at Larry, but he didn't look as if he realized how I actually felt. He was probably just remarking in general. If I didn't reply, he might think something was funny, so I said, "Yup."

"Yup," said Larry again, "I really admire that girl. Hell of a lot of talent, brains and as good-looking as she is nice. You were in the Army with her brother, right?"

"Marines," I corrected dispassionately.

"Same thing. You all three went to war together: only he got killed. She says he thought a lot of you guys, one hell of a lot. Course, that shows or she wouldn't be here. She said he was right when he wrote her that he had found the perfect man for her, even if the dude was white. A really sharp guy who was also a man and who would take care of her right. She said all she has to do now is pull the guy's head out of the sky so he'll notice her as a woman and not a member of The Group or Frank's sister."

Whomp! fell the bomb on my head. *Bang!* went the explosion. *Thump!* went my heart as it hit the floor. *Phui* went my soul as it flew away to the land of the lost.

I looked at Meredith laughing and earnestly talking to Donnely at the table and almost cried, but I didn't. I turned to Larry and said, "Yeah, Frank was right. The perfect man."

One thing I should point out in the midst of these painful memories: At this time all anybody in The Group—except Donnely and maybe the Professor—knew was that we were going to rob a bank. What bank, where, when and how, nobody knew. The reason I think maybe the Professor knew is his telegram started the whole thing.

The telegram was full of nonsense. The signature was the key: "Erato."

For those of you, like me, to whom the name Erato means little or nothing, let me introduce you to her. Erato, whose name means literally "lovesome," was the muse of erotic poetry. She and her eight sister muses were the inspiring goddesses of song and divinities presiding over poetry, the arts and the sciences in Greek mythology. Got that?

The fact that there are nine muses eventually led me to deduce that The Plan had originally considered nine possible banks to rob, with Erato eventually being chosen as the one.

Of course, I didn't figure this out until much later, a long time after I handed Donnely the telegram. His eyes glistened when he saw it and he retired into the bedroom he used as his office. An hour later he emerged to tell me to track down the rest of The Group and bring them to the headquarters apartment as soon as possible.

I found all of them. Meredith (whom I went looking for

first) was at the zoo taking pictures of animals. I have always liked animals, but I didn't tell her that.

Alfred and Larry weren't far away. They were trying a slightly modified Gamathon Fertility Ray on a female gorilla. They didn't want the species to die out. They like animals, too. Reginald was studying people for future characterizations. He watched them from the corner a block from Hollywood and Vine. Raoul took a little finding, but I eventually tracked him down to the bedroom of, you guessed it, a tanned, blond, hopeful starlet. I used a technique he taught me to pick the front door lock and I entered the bedroom just seconds before the afternoon's activities were to reach a crescendo. Normally I would have waited a few minutes until they were finished, but I didn't want Raoul exhausted when The Plan was starting. So I opened the bedroom door and yelled, "Picture!" hoping to stop the action before all of Raoul's energy was spent. The blonde responded like a true performer and froze. Raoul wasn't particularly happy with me, but he came along anyway.

Donnely was waiting for us when we got back. When we were all seated, he spoke. I'm going to leave out the background noises of Raoul's radio and Larry's mumblings, but you remember they were there.

"This is it," Donnely said, "we're starting the active part of Phase one."

Now I should have stopped the whole thing to ask some questions, right after that statement. But the implications it contained went over my excited head.

"I have written instructions for each of you and have put them in envelopes," Donnely continued. "You'll find them on the desk in my office. Follow them exactly to the letter and don't tell anyone your assignment. If you do that, you will automatically try to piece things together and at this stage that could be bad. It would mean you would have to 'unlearn' your speculations when we have the details of The Plan, so watch your imagination, too, at least for now.

"Meredith, I'll pick you up in half an hour at your apartment. I assume you've kept a bag packed like I told you

44

to and all your equipment is in order. We have to leave for a while, probably about three days. While I'm gone, Jack is in charge. Any questions?"

I didn't like it. I didn't mind being in charge, but him going off with Meredith for three days. . . . Oh, well, I thought, from what Larry said it had been pretty much decided already. I tried to bring myself to wish her good luck, but I'm not that unselfish.

I don't know what the others got for instructions, but I know what mine said; "Go buy a conservative dark gray suit, a white shirt and a plain black tie with the enclosed money. Also get a pair of black wingtip shoes. And a haircut, a little bit longer than a crew cut. Wear the clothes enough so they don't look new. Be sure and break in the shoes. Also, keep things cool. I'll call if I need to, and if any problems come up you can't handle, wire the Professor at the address on his telegram. I don't expect to hear from you. Donnely."

That was it. I thought everything sounded kind of stupid, but I did it anyway.

Four mornings later—three long, sleepless nights—Donnely and Meredith came back. I barely had time to greet an eager Meredith before she disappeared into the bedroom at headquarters which we had converted into a darkroom. Donnely also seemed very eager. He disappeared into the other bedroom, the one he used as his office. I rounded up the others.

That morning was hectic, a little like opening night for the blond starlets. Reginald, acting on instructions and assisted by Meredith, applied complicated makeup (including false ears) for all of us. Raoul, Donnely, Reginald and I received cheek pads, scars, moles, skin dyes and other things, depending on the individual. Then Meredith took portrait pictures of four of us: Reginald, Donnely and I wore our new clothes and Raoul wore a shirt with numbers over the left pocket. Meredith disappeared into the darkroom again and I went home to change back to normal clothes. By the time I returned things had calmed down to maternity ward level excitement.

We waited two more hours for the announcement of the birth. It took Meredith an hour and thirty minutes of that time to finish whatever she was doing in the darkroom. The last half hour she spent in the office—I couldn't forget it was a bedroom—with Donnely. She came out beaming and set up an easel, just like the kind the officers used to brief us in the Marines.

When Donnely emerged to join us, I was so excited I forgot to be jealous. He put a stack of papers on the easel, some of them poster size. The top sheet was a map, and I could see the edges of blown-up photographs behind it.

"Gentlemen and lady," he said with a gracious bow to Meredith, "the time has come, the hour has sprung, and we are ready to begin holding up the bank.

"This," he said, gesturing to the map, "is a map of the northwestern corner of Arizona, the area bordering both Utah and Nevada. More precisely, the area surrounding Hamilton, Arizona, a new prosperous community of fifty thousand citizens, most of them wealthy senior citizens basking in the golden glow of the twilight years.

"You will receive a copy of this map, a map of Hamilton itself, a highway map of the area and copies of all reconnaissance photos and drawings in your individual packets. Memorize every detail so that you could draw them if you had to, and you will have to because you will be tested on them."

Donnely removed the map to show a large photograph of a sprawling one-story brick-and-glass building on a busy main street. The architect obviously believed in openness, for almost all the bank's walls were long, story-high windows, allowing you to see inside the bank. I happened to notice that one of the cars parked a little ways from the bank was a police cruiser. That didn't look good.

"This," continued Donnely, just like he was speaking to the Chamber of Commerce, "is the First State Citizens' Bank of Hamilton, Arizona, the largest of six banks in the town. The town also has three savings and loan associations. This bank's normal assets are approximately two point seven nine million dollars."

46

"I say normal because at certain times of the year the bank has cash assets which alone exceed one million dollars. Three weeks from now will be one of those times.

"A combination of fortuitous events will cause the bank to have on hand approximately one point five million dollars in cash with denominations ranging from one-dollar to hundred-dollar bills, all old, all with unrecorded serial numbers. The bank will also have on hand approximately half a million in recorded dollars of the same denominations.

"There are several major circumstances which have combined to bring this money to Hamilton's leading bank, three of which I think you should know.

"One. Hamilton is not far from the gambling of Las Vegas. Many of Hamilton's citizens have a good deal of money and like to flit over the border and try to get Lady Luck to come across with just a little more before they go to the great gambling room in the sky. Credit card devices are not as romantic as cold, hard cash, or as accepted for those activities. Consequently the bank keeps a large supply of cash on hand to serve its commuting customers. This is a given, a condition which put the bank under consideration for The Plan in the first place.

"Two. The Federal Reserve Bank in Arizona is moving a large shipment of new bills into the Nevada area for distribution to the general public. The dispersal point at which Nevada banks are going to pick up their allotted new dollars to distribute is, of course, our bank in Hamilton. This dispersal is scheduled for two days after we hit the bank and was the deciding factor in choosing this particular bank for The Plan.

"Three, and most important, Apollo Industries, Inc., a Swiss company which as yet exists only on paper and which, I might add, you are all substantial stockholders in and future employees of, has announced its intention to open a branch plant in Hamilton. Now Apollo has established an old fashioned method of doing business: It pays in cash. So the payrolls for the construction crews, the Apollo Industries' staff and the bill collectors who will surely gather around must be in cash. Consequently, the bank which gleefully

47

handles the Apollo account must keep an inordinately large amount of cash on hand. Naturally, Apollo Industries banks at the First State Citizens' Bank and naturally the first Apollo payroll is due the day before the dispersal of the new federal money. Naturally, the bank is increasing its cash on hand.

"So that, fellow Group members, is the bank.

"And this," said Donnely, leaning forward eagerly, "is how we are going to get them to give us the money."

The Pull-Off

Ties make my neck itch. It doesn't make any difference how loose I wear them, my neck still itches. I know it's caused by the sweat on my collar and not the ties, but I don't like to wear them anyway, partially because they make my neck itch, partially because I'm always getting them caught in something and partially because I think they're stupid in the first place. They especially make my neck itch when it's hot out or when I'm nervous. So you can imagine how my neck felt surrounded by a tie and a stiff white collar in the Arizona heat on the way to hold up a bank. But I had to just grin and bear it because FBI agents are tough and if anybody suspected I wasn't an FBI agent, I might be running from some real G-men.

I suppose I should back up a little. The memory of me nervously grinning and bearing it while riding in the car with the Hamilton chief of police, Officer Hodgson with his riot gun, Reginald and Donnely on the way to hold up the bank is a kind of unfair place to drop you in at all of a sudden. So I'll back up a bit.

Donnely's Plan was indeed a masterpiece, a beaut. It is so good I'm not sure how to start describing it to you. If you remember all I have already told you, you'll know he had been laying the groundwork for the actual robbery for years.

The plan was simplicity in itself. Bank robberies, in these days of electronic security systems, private guards, excellent police communications systems and an omnipresent FBI, are seldom successful. Donnely deduced that the reason so few modern bank robberies work is the method used by the robbers—*i.e.*, they take the money from the bank by force. So his Plan was to have the bank give us the money.

Simple, huh? Exactly how we got them to give us the money comes later. First some background details.

The move from LA to Hamilton was done quietly, in stages. Donnely had set a cover (including a disguise) for Meredith as the advance representative of a nonexistent movie company. Under that guise she acquired many things for us, including a house with a large garage and an apartment overlooking the bank. The week before the operation we spent practicing our various tasks and roles. Two days before the pull-off we actually began work.

We planned the holdup for a Friday when bank employees and police would be thinking of the weekend. When the robbery made them shift their concentration back to their business duties, they would (we hoped) be more susceptible to excitement and confusion.

On Wednesday an official-looking green telephone truck pulled up behind the bank and a lineman scurried up the pole to check the terminal boxes. All the other telephone trucks in town were at the opposite end of the city, repairing extensive damage done by some "unknown" pranksters the night before. While Larry made the necessary adjustments in the terminal, I stood on the ground by the newly purchased and disguised van, trying to look official. I also tried to avoid looking at the bank and our apartment, which was just visible over the bank's roof. Alfred was in that apartment now, monitoring the instruments he and Larry had perfected during the week.

To show you how thorough Donnely's plan was, Raoul, posing as a special delivery mailman, was at that moment quietly dropping official forms into the Work Completed basket at the phone company, just in case anybody from the bank or the police called to check. Raoul had stolen those forms the week before, using the same disguise.

I might point out that in all our operation forays we were disguised, each time slightly differently and each time drilled in our roles by the head casting director, Reginald. Even

50

Meredith wore disguises, although I didn't see how anyone could ever mistake her having once seen her in any form.

After we rigged the bank's phones, we drove to the city-county jail terminal box and rigged the police phones. Then we rigged the terminals behind a restaurant and a certain house in the suburban flats.

Thursday night or, more correctly, 4:02 Friday morning, Raoul and I paid a visit to the resident FBI agent's suburban house. He didn't have a dog or any kids, which was a lucky break for us. We picked the lock and quietly entered the house. Lulling music came softly from Raoul's transistor radio. The FBI agent and his wife never realized they had been gassed with the special sleeping gas Alfred, Meredith and Larry whipped up. I know it works and is harmless because they used it on me as an experiment. I got fourteen hours of uninterrupted, blissful sleep. So did the agent and his wife.

In the hours following the mission to the agent's house the Group consumed uncounted cups of coffee. At 7 A.M. we all ate a high-energy, high-protein breakfast and, after nervous wishes of good luck, went to our respective assignments.

Dressed in our special suits and ties and carrying exact but harmless replicas of the .38 revolvers issued the FBI (Donnely insisted on realism and nonviolence), Donnely, Reginald and I drove our newly purchased, slightly modified black Ford sedan to the police station. In carefully worn plastic folders were beautifully forged ID cards certifying that we were indeed agents of the Federal Bureau of Investigation. We made Reginald the chief inspector, partially because he is the oldest and partially because he is the best. He relished every minute of it.

At 9:15, after having taken the police chief and his best officer (with his pet riot gun) home to change into civilian clothes, we sat in the office of Morris Sylvester, the fat, heavy-jowled president of the First State Citizens' Bank of Hamilton, Arizona, explaining "the situation." Or rather Reginald—*i.e.,* "Inspector Eprad Schwartz"—was explaining "the situation."

"I must admit, Mr. Sylvester, that I am somewhat hampered and confused by the urgency this case requires. My agents and I have also been spending a lot of hard hours piecing this thing together, so if I seem to wander or skip a few points. . . ."

President Sylvester interrupted as if he knew the script. "Oh, no, inspector, you're quite clear, quite clear. But you haven't told me yet why you and Chief Parker—and of course your assistants—have come here this morning."

Reginald gave him his best man-to-man smile. "Let me be blunt, Mr. Sylvester. We have every reason to believe that some time today your bank will be held up."

"Oh, dear me!" President Sylvester paled considerably.

"Furthermore," continued Reginald, "we intend to let it happen. We want it to happen."

"Oh, dear, dear me!" President Sylvester's jowls trembled.

"Let me explain. For the last four months my group and I have been on the trail of a very successful, very dangerous gang of bank robbers. They have held up banks in three states, always using the same MO. That's bureau phrasing for *modus operandi*, in case you didn't know.

"The way the gang operates is this: They pick a town in which a bank is going to have a large amount of cash on hand. Then they do two things. They compromise a low-level bank official and a low-level police official. Sometimes they use blackmail; sometimes they kidnap a wife or husband; sometimes they bribe. At any rate, they gain a set of eyes and ears within the bank and within the police department. With this advantage and a blitzkrieg holdup method, they know when, where and how to hit the bank. Their insiders keep them informed of all activities before and after the robbery so the gang can elude capture and justice."

"Oh, my!" President Sylvester's vocabulary is very limited. He should spend some time in prison.

"Yes. So far they have eluded us, but not for much longer. For one thing, we've been able to positively identify at least one of the gang. This man, Thomas Dewey."

Reginald handed the president two mug shots of Raoul made up and wearing his numbered shirt. The president

52

took them with a trembling hand, glanced at them quickly, then thrust them back.

"I have never seen that man in my entire life," said Sylvester defensively.

"We know," replied Chameleon-Inspector Schwartz-Reginald, "but our local resident agent has. He spotted him outside your bank yesterday afternoon, called us and we drove up from Phoenix last night. We're sure they're going to hit you today because they never come into the town until the day before the holdup.

"Unfortunately, when we arrived in town we found our local agent had been unable to tell the chief about the holdup. The chief called the agent at home and his wife said he was extremely ill with strep throat. The wife read us a message he wrote just before the doctor sedated and medicated him."

The "wife" of course, was Meredith. Right then she, Raoul, Alfred and Larry were sitting in the apartment at a massive switchboard, monitoring all calls going in and out of the FBI agent's house, the bank and the police department. They also had a police radio and a radio monitoring the listening devices we three "agents" carried.

"Well, then," said Sylvester, "why don't you stop these bandits from holding up my bank? It's your duty!" Sylvester punched his desk with a pudgy fist.

"We'd like to," continued Reginald, "and we could. But that would defeat our purpose, to say nothing of possibly endangering innocent lives [like our own, I thought]. You see, we think we know who some of the gang are, but we don't know who the mastermind is, and it's him we want to catch. So we have a plan.

"The thieves always use the same sacks the money is in at the bank to haul the money away. The money then goes to the mastermind, who makes sure it isn't chemically treated, and he distributes it back to the gang. We are going to plant electronic devices in the bags of money here at the bank, let the crooks take them and then follow the homing signal to the mastermind and their headquarters. That way we can nab the whole lot."

"But what if it fails? What if something goes wrong? Then what?" Sylvester was definitely worried.

"That's why we're going to let them only take the new money, the money with the serial numbers on record. If you like, you can check with the Federal Reserve Bank in Phoenix and they'll verify that my plan is OK." '

This, of course, was a well-backed bluff. If Sylvester had called the Federal Bank, his call would have been intercepted and he would have talked to Alfred, who, in his best Shakespearean voice, sounds just like the president of the Phoenix Federal Reserve Bank.

Sylvester didn't call the bluff, but he did get cagey. "You said the gang compromises a bank employee and a low-level police officer. How do you know you can trust myself, Chief Parker or Officer Hodgson?"

Reginald smiled. "Because our agent had time to check all of you out yesterday before he became too ill to move. That was what his wife told us."

"Oh." You could see Sylvester was worried about what our "agent" had found. "I see. Well, all right. What is it exactly that you want us to do?"

Reginald immediately slipped into his commanding general role.

"First, distribute the new recorded bills to the tellers for their use. Second, leave the unused portions in the sacks and put the sacks in the unlocked vault. Agents Lawrence and Killman"—Reginald nodded at Donnely and me—"will bug the sacks. Third, we are going to transfer the bulk of your remaining cash supply to a motel near here where the chief, Officer Hodgson and myself will guard it until after the robbery. Last but not least, you must tell no one what is going on except those few tellers who will help pack the money and your head cashier. He was also cleared by our local agent. Chief Parker, likewise, has told only Officer Hodgson, so the insider in his department has no way of knowing The Plan. I must also insist you keep the tellers who pack the money locked in your office with yourself and on no account should they or you leave or telephone. Your option on this is to lock

54

them in here yourself, rip out the phone and go with the money."

"Oh, I had better do that," Sylvester said quickly. "The trustees would want me to stay with the money."

"All right," said Reginald. "Shall we get started? I'm afraid we may not have much time. The gang usually strikes about two."

Have you ever tried to pack three-quarters of a million dollars? It took the ten of us, Sylvester, Chief Parker, Officer Hodgson (without his riot gun), the three Group members, the head cashier and three clerks an hour and a half to pack all that money into hastily, secretly procured suitcases, boxes and bags. We worked in the vault. Sylvester staved off curiosity by explaining that we were CPA trainees practicing counting money and helping the police look for counterfeit currency which had been reported in the area. It was a fishy story, but the employees believed their president. At least, they didn't question him.

At 10:47 the last paper sack was crammed into the station wagon Donnely had been sent to rent. Actually, of course, he merely walked to the parking lot where he had stashed it, waited the appropriate amount of time, then drove it to the bank. At 11:07 Inspector Schwartz (Reginald), Chief Parker (in desperate need of a toilet), Officer Hodgson (cradling his riot gun in the back seat) and President Sylvester (continually mopping his brow with a handkerchief) drove to the motel.

Of course, they never went to the motel. As they circled the block "to come in the back way," Reginald, who had been building up his endurance all week, took a deep breath and pushed the button which automatically closed the windows, locked the doors and filled the car with sleeping gas. Larry's modifications worked to perfection. In that small an area the gas takes slightly over ten seconds to work. Twenty seconds later Reginald pulled the car into the garage behind our rented house, shut off the engine and dashed for pure air. He made it.

Two minutes later he returned to the car; only this time he had Larry, who had driven from the apartment, to help him.

They wore gas masks. They gently extracted the sleeping officials, tied them up and drove the aired money-ladened station wagon to the rendezvous point.

And what were Donnely and I doing all this time? Sitting in the bank, waiting for the little electronic tingle to come through the receivers strapped to our thighs and tell us everything was under control.

At 11:46 we got that tingle. Donnely looked at me and smiled. I couldn't help smiling back. We were halfway there!

We were sitting with the nervous head cashier behind his partition. We could see the customers through a one-way glass, but they couldn't see us. Donnely stretched, yawned and said, "I think I'll take lunch now, Agent Killman, if that's OK with you. We shouldn't have any action until two anyway."

I said that was fine, he told us what restaurant he was going to, we looked up and wrote down the phone number, and out he went.

I chatted nervously with the cashier until 12:10. He was so nervous I don't think he noticed I shook, too. Then I got another little tingle.

Five minutes later a slick-haired, snappy-suited, elevator-shoed, scar-faced character who looked not at all like Raoul strolled into the bank, his body shuffling in time to a barely audible, unseen transistor radio. I pointed him out to the head cashier.

"Look, it's the guy in the picture we've identified as a gang member! He's early, probably casing the joint one last time."

The cashier nodded numbly and swallowed hard. As he pushed the button which would take the suspect's picture (a waste of film), I picked up the phone, once again thankful that FBI agents do not shake hands. If they did, the people we met that day might have noticed all the agents had on surgeons' thin plastic gloves. We would leave no fingerprints. As radio station KOMA announced another dynamite *Beatle Blast from Out of the Past!* I dialed the restaurant number.

My call was, of course, intercepted by Meredith, the only one left in the apartment. She didn't pay any attention as I informed Agent Lawrence of the new development. In the pause she said, "Jack, listen to me. Everything is going according to plan. Remember that. And, Jack, please be careful. Both of you. For me. Please tell Donnely that I said he was to be very careful. OK?"

I suppose my ears reddened, but I said, "I understand, Agent Lawrence. Over and out." I hung up the phone unnecessarily hard, but she was probably already on her way to the rendezvous.

"Agent Lawrence agrees with me that the guy is doing a recon job," I told the cashier. "I'm going to follow him when he leaves and Agent Lawrence will pick him up outside, just in case he spots me. I hate to leave you alone, but this way we'll be right on top of them when they hit the place. Any questions?"

The cashier nervously shook his head no.

I smiled and clapped him on the shoulder. "Brace up, everything will be OK just as long as you follow the plan. Remember, don't tell anyone what's going on. We don't want to show our hand." Then I reached in my coat pocket and pushed a buzzer which electronically signaled Raoul to leave the bank. I followed him, trying my best to look like J. Edgar Hoover. Raoul went straight for two blocks, then turned left, headed for Alfred's pickup and the rendezvous. I turned right when I reached the corner, walked a block and climbed into the passenger seat of the black Ford. Donnely put it in gear and away we went.

The Pushover

I giggled and laughed during the whole drive. First we stopped at the house. After checking the sleeping prisoners, we changed our disguises and put everything in a plastic garbage bag. The house had already been cleaned out, but we went over it again anyway. Next we went to the apartment, casually checking out the bank on the way. Everything looked OK. It took awhile to dismantle the remaining electrical equipment in the apartment. We finished at 2:45, fifteen minutes before the end of the banking day. We made it to the city dump by 3:05. We ditched the police radio just as a call went out for the chief of police and a squad car to report to the First State Citizens' Bank. The cashier must have guessed something was wrong. By the time we got back to town sirens from police cars converging on the bank could be heard a mile away. We whipped into a McDonald's. Donnely sent me in to order while he used the pay phone outside to make sure everyone was at the rendezvous point. I didn't know where that was.

I suppose the waitresses thought I was crazy, whistling, singing and forcing a dollar tip on them. I watched through the window as Donnely made the call. Then, oddly, he made another call. He turned in the booth and flashed me the OK sign and I grinned back. We had done it!

Donnely, for some strange reason, insisted on eating there instead of on the way to the rendezvous. Since he was driving, I couldn't argue. We giggled and laughed and Donnely asked me if I still believed in long-term investments and temporary sacrifice as opposed to immediate short-term gain. A man and a woman pushing a baby buggy stopped in front of the McDonald's. I said sure. I would have said sure to about anything right then. A carload of old freaky-looking dudes pulled up along our left side. Donnely said that was good and took a bite of his Big Mac. A bored-looking businessman carrying a briefcase got out of a car and started walking toward the litter barrel in front of our car. I took a sip of my chocolate milk shake. The bored-looking businessman dropped his briefcase. All hell broke loose.

Suddenly there was a police cruiser behind us, lights flashing and sirens blaring! The cop in the driver's seat had his revolver trained on us! I dropped my milk shake in my lap! The bored-looking businessman who had dropped his briefcase now held a huge .44 magnum pointed right at me through the windshield! The carload of freaks to our left now held riot guns pointed you-know-where and the man and the woman with the baby buggy cradled cute little machine pistol "grease guns" aimed toward your humble narrator!

Before they pulled us from the car and dragged us away to the police station, I had time to look at Donnely. He smiled reassuringly and that made me have to ask it, although I had an awful fear I already knew the answer.

"How? How did they find us?"

My door was jerked open and a voice yelled, "Come out with your hands high!" but I managed to hear Donnely's reply.

Quite calmly he said, "I called them."

PHASE II

The Preliminaries

My cell was exactly five and a half paces wide and seven and a half paces long, with "long" running parallel to the corridor. It contained two cots, one mine and the other one vacant (until they assigned me a roommate), a sink, a toilet without a flapping seat so I couldn't commit suicide or other mayhem and two chairs, steel and bolted to the floor. A small slate folded up from the bottom of each chair, just like the old school desks in my college days. The slate was big enough to play a game of solitaire on or to balance a small checkerboard. The edges of the slate were rounded, like all the exposed edges in my steel room, so I couldn't slit my wrists. A small metal chest was bolted to the floor at the foot of each bed. I kept my clean and dirty clothes there and a few books. I also kept a picture of Donnely, Frank Douglas and myself because I didn't have a picture of Meredith and would have been afraid to display it even if I had one for fear of incriminating her. Three of my cell walls were concrete; one was not. It had steel bars and the steel bar door which locked both manually and electronically. The wall opposite the barred wall and hall had a small window in it, eleven feet off the floor. If you jumped that high, you found nothing to hold onto, because the shatterproof, bulletproof glass was flush with the wall.

Let me direct you to my cell: First, go to Havensbrook Federal Penitentiary. There you must pass under massive stone walls through the locked gate to the inner driveway. They will shut the gate behind you. Next, you pass through the heavy iron gated main entrance. They will shut the door behind you. Then, if you still have permission to continue, you must leave your vehicle and walk through first one steel door, then another. They will shut them behind you. Both doors can't be opened at the same time. If you were a prisoner, they would strip and search you in between those two doors. If you're not, they usually just lightly frisk you by hand and with metal detectors. Then they will let you through the second door and you must walk across the courtyard to my cellblock. The sniper guards on the walls will watch you all the way. You will be able to hear the dogs in the pens growling at you. Screws might check you before they let you in the locked cellblock door. They will shut it behind you. They might check you after you get inside, too. Next, you must walk through to the locked door leading to the cells. When you pass through that door, they will shut it behind you. You will walk down the halls with your guard ("escort," if you're not a prisoner), climb the stairs to the second floor, walk down the steel corridor and face my cell. The guard-escort will manually unlock the door and nod to the floor guard, who sits enclosed in a bulletproof glass cage. The floor guard must throw the switch electronically unlocking the seventy-four-pound door to my cell. You, not the guard-escort, must slide it back, step inside, shut it. After it locks electronically, the guard-escort locks it manually; *et voilà*, there you are.

My cell had five colors: gray for walls, bunk and metal objects. White for the sink, toilet and bed sheets. Black for the bars. Green for the blankets on the bed. Blue for my clothes. And me. My cell had two smells. One was pine-scented disinfectant. The other was hate for Daniel James Donnely. There was no hope smell. My cell had one predominant sound echoing through it: men in varying stages of physical and psychological pain.

Now it probably isn't very fair to introduce you to Phase II by dropping you smack dab in the middle of my cell without any kind of lead-in. It probably isn't very pleasant either, but then think how I felt when I found myself there.

I'll back up a little.

Besides us, the police found a packet of the marked bills in the black sedan's jockey box. I've never known why it's called a jockey box. I think the label is a misnomer because no jockey, no matter how good he was, could fit in there and still be big enough to ride a horse. Needless to say, the discovery of the money came as a big surprise to me. Donnely must have hidden it there before I met him in the car. However, I didn't tell the police, the FBI or the public prosecutor that. I didn't tell them anything because I was afraid they would work something out of me which would endanger the rest of The Group and Meredith. At least I could protect her.

I also thought about killing Donnely. When they kept yelling questions at me hour after hour, I ignored them by conjuring up visions of how I would make him die.

But with the black sedan identified by an angry police chief, a disgusted bank president and a slightly insane Officer Hodgson (they had to sedate him to keep him from using his riot gun on us), plus the presence of stolen bills in my immediate possession, plus the fact that Donnely confessed that we had done it (he refused to say anything else. If he had told on Meredith and the others, I would have fought my way through the concrete jail to kill him), plus the fact that my lawyer (??—that's what I thought too) pleaded me guilty, my fate was only a question of time.

At my sentencing I found out I had waived the right to a preliminary hearing and I discovered both Donnely and I were represented by J. Bartholomew Muckleston, attorney at and professor of law. You've heard of him as the Professor.

J. Bartholomew Muckleston is probably the most famous unfamous attorney in the nation, if not the world. Although he has never formally taught, he deserves his title of Professor, for he is dean of American legal scholarship. The Professor's office sits behind the drugstore in Beaver Crossing, Nebraska. It's a one-man practice and his only assistant is a local high school girl gaining office experience as part of her business class. Each year the Professor must break in a new girl, but since the secretary's major chores are dusting, filing and typing, the rapid turnover rate causes him few problems.

The Professor hasn't always practiced out of his Beaver

Crossing office. Until 1969 he worked out of his own legal factory with offices in New York, Chicago, Los Angeles, Houston, London and Paris. The firm's headquarters were in Delaware, the first state admitted to the Union and coincidentally one of the easiest and least demanding states for corporate operations. Every major U.S. corporation worth its weight in stock certificates retained the Professor as a connivance consultant. He helped the corporations hide their assets from taxation, protect their products from regulation, mask their pollution behind waivers and variances, disguise their real owners and in general operate free of government "interference." His contracts are on par with those of the devil and some say Lucifer did an earthly stint as one of his numerous law clerks (the Professor operated without partners). The Professor's methods for dealing with torts and suits rarely brought clients less than twice what they expected in their wildest dreams. He once wrote an appellate brief for a client (who shall remain nameless) that forced the U.S. Supreme Court to abuse and buffet the brief's clear language, penetrating arguments and astounding scholarship, deleting whole sections before the court issued it as its own unanimous opinion. The damage had to be done or no one would have believed the Court had arrived at its own decision: The brief was too good. That same year one of the Professor's roses won a blue ribbon at the Delaware State Fair. The ribbon hangs over his bed. A laudatory letter from the Supreme Court is somewhere in his attic.

Right now you might be asking yourself, "If this guy was so good, how come I've never heard of him?" If that question raised itself in your mind, then you really don't know much about the practice of law in America. The people who do know the perpetual play of jurisprudence know about the Professor, despite his efforts to maintain as low a profile as possible. Selective anonymity is one of the Professor's better tools and shyness is one of his strongest traits.

The Professor didn't particularly like finagling for rapacious corporations, but everyone has to make a living and, as the old legal maxim notes, "Justice doesn't pay." The Professor balanced reality with utopia by refusing to use his full efforts to circumvent the law and the myths of a just, egalitarian America. The man has a highly developed social conscience. But his competitive drive is almost as highly developed. The Professor worked for his clients because they paid him well for the most challenging legal work he could find. While the government isn't particularly adept at regulating the money players, Uncle Sam is still a formidable opponent, if for no other reason than his sheer bulk and complexity. The Professor found his perpetual struggles with our good government a pleasant, invigorating challenge to his single-handed efforts. His conscience kept him from completely defeating his opponent. With the government to satisfy his competitive drive, his self-imposed restraint to salve his conscience and the lucrative fees of his clients to satisfy his less esoteric needs, the Professor was a contented man.

But not a happy man. While the challenge and rewards of his practice amused the Professor, he suffered because he failed to find fulfillment in his career. The Professor never really wanted to be a lawyer. His one true passion in life had always been gardening. Even at the height of his corporate practice the fate of his plants stood foremost in his mind. A major steel company president loves to tell how the Professor used every trick in the book to force a delay in the trial of an antipollution suit against the steel mills simply because the closet cultivator wanted to be in Delaware when his lilacs bloomed.

The Professor's mother, a tenacious, long-lived, matriarchal tyrant, decided the Professor's fate early in his life. She wasn't going to have her hard-earned, Harvard-spent dollars squandered on a son who wanted to be a botanist. So the Professor made the best of his situation by becoming the greatest behind-the-scenes attorney in the world and gardening on the side.

The day his mother was buried, the Professor left the firm which he had founded and retired to Nebraska to devote most of his efforts to gardening. More than a desire to revel in passion prompted his move; He was finding law duller by

67

the day. When you can beat the government whenever you want, what challenge is left? Ralph Nader is spread too thin to be formidable. The Professor maintained a law office in Beaver Crossing solely out of habit, curiosity and inertia, refusing virtually all the hundreds of wealthy clients who wore down paths to his office door.

I don't know where Donnely heard about the Professor, but then much of Donnely's knowledge is a mystery to me. Donnely didn't go to the Professor's office. One fine May morning the Professor found Donnely carefully weeding the three-acre garden *behind* the Professor's office. They spent the day together under the Beaver Crossing sun, talking, working in the earth and discussing life in general. Donnely told the Professor about The Plan over dinner, and after receiving assurances that fine gardens could be grown in states besides Nebraska, the Professor joined The Group. He was eager for new challenges, and Donnely and The Plan gave him unexperienced horizons without restraining his passions.

Evidently the word had traveled across the bar that the Old Man (a fairly accurate description of the Professor since he is sixty-seven) was actually defending clients in a criminal case, a sensational criminal case no less. The courtroom was packed with every famous and almost famous lawyer in the land. A Supreme Court Justice wanted to come, but he was afraid his presence at the trial might disqualify him if our case were appealed. The Justice didn't want to do that, so he settled for sending his law clerk with a movie camera and tape recorder.

I suppose the lawyers were all disappointed. The Professor, looking more like a misplaced hayseed in his sloppy, rack-purchased blue suit, said very little. When the judge asked him if he had a presentation to make, the Professor merely requested the judge to read his submitted written brief carefully.

Evidently the judge did so, for the Professor was satisfied with the ruling. I was told we had made a deal to plead guilty on a state bank-robbing charge. Other charges (such as im-

68

personating a federal officer, kidnapping, federal bank robbery charges, etc.) were dropped.

The Professor and Donnely might have been satisfied with the ruling, but I wasn't. I don't suppose thirty years without parole seemed like too much to two geniuses, but I knew that was my life. I had to be restrained from attacking Donnely. He just shook his head and said, "Jack, think about it. I'll talk to you later."

I'd think about it all right. Like for thirty years I'd think about it. And when "later" came, I knew exactly what I was going to say or, rather, do. I was going to strangle the mother.

A funny thing happened right after they handcuffed me to my chair and the courtroom settled down.

The judge cleared his throat and said, "I have here a rather curious motion from the defense counsel." The audience of lawyers stirred in eager anticipation of The Greatest Lawyer's coup which they knew was coming. The judge continued. "It seems both defendants suffer from a condition of *allergic rhinitis,* a condition partially brought on by their service in Vietnam. Medical certification is duly attached and the Court accepts it as valid and true.

"On the basis of this accepted condition, defense counsel requests that any long-term incarceration of the defendants be done at the new federal penitentiary, Havensbrook. The climatic conditions at Havensbrook, according to defense counsel's brief, are such that the defendants will not suffer cruel and unusual punishment through aggravations brought on by their allergenic condition. Defense counsel notes that this might not be the case at any other prison and such imposition of cruel and unusual punishment might constitute basis for subsequent appeal. The defense counsel also points out that the new library at Havensbrook will enable defendant Donnely to continue his education and may help improve the mind of defendant Mason." The judge paused.

"I would like to say at this time that this request, while not without precedent in jurisprudence, is a mild surprise. However, the Court can find no fault, direct or implied, in the request and considering the defendants' admitted plea, the gravity of the crime, the impeccable correctness of the defense brief and"—the judge paused to smile at the Professor. The judge had gone to Harvard—"the fine legal reputation of defense counsel, the Court finds this request well taken and so orders the sentencing."

The galleries cheered as if the Professor had won an acquittal. They didn't know what they were cheering for and neither did I. I did see the Professor wink at Donnely and then Donnely, the SOB, used his forefinger and thumb to flash me the same OK sign he flashed me from the phone booth outside the McDonald's.

I raised my manacled hand as high as I could and flashed him a sign with my middle finger.

I suppose you are wondering about that allergy bit. I guess it came from the physical Donnely made all of us take. I answered the doctor's questions truthfully. Cats make me sneeze.

I also suppose you're wondering about the other members of The Group. At that time, so was I. I knew they had gotten away and I was glad for them. I desperately wanted to know how Meredith was, but the Professor wouldn't tell me. He said to wait.

Sure, I'd wait. Thirty years.

The next day they took us to Havensbrook. The last I saw of Donnely (for a while) was the cheerful wave he gave me as they led him away to his cell.

The other night I saw an old James Cagney prison picture on television and I had to laugh. I also had to cry. Maybe I should tell you a little bit about Havensbrook Federal Penitentiary, or Heaven as the cons in stir there call it.

Havensbrook is the newest maximum-security federal pen in the country. They stuck it in the middle of nowhere, just northeast of the Grand Canyon and just west of Black Mesa, an area the Indians hold sacred. I heard the power companies are going to build on the mesa, so the ghosts in the area should become shockers in a little while, and if capital punishment ever becomes chic again, it will be a cheap thrill for

Arizona taxpayers because they won't have far to funnel the joy juice.

Havensbrook opened in 1972 as a place to keep naughty people out of sight and out of mind. They tell me that as prisons go, it's pretty modern. I mean it has toilets and not mason jars like the ones the federal women's pen used until 1968. I suppose there are worse places to spend thirty years of your life, although I'm not sure I could name them.

Since the object is to keep the inmates out of sight and mind, if that is accomplished, nothing else matters. Havensbrook is a classic closed society and in many ways a model mirror image of the prisons most people imagine.

There are two types of people behind Havensbrook's massive gray stone walls at any one time, the keepers and the kept. The keepers are the guards, officers, civilian clerks and assistants, and wardens, all of whom are generally known as screws. The pecking order of prestige and power in this group is determined pretty much by obvious, classic methods like salaries, titles, etc. The other group of people are the kept, the cons.

Among the cons there are two separate societies, those who have clout and those who don't. What's clout? A con from Chicago explained it to me like this:

"Clout is when you know somebody or are a part of something that can do things. I mean that can *really* do things, that has real power. Clout means you count, you're somebody. Like in Chi, I got a clout down at City Hall who fixes parking tickets for me. I know a heist artist who has clout with his local precinct. My ward boss, he don't got no clout with the Machine, which is bad, because in Chicago, the Machine owns almost all the clout there is, or at least what the Syndicate don't own."

Understand clout? OK, now let's talk about Havensbrook. About forty percent of the cons have clout of varying degrees. A small example is the pickpocket who used to work the Capitol building in D.C. and got caught boosting from a Senator. That con's rating comes from knowing and being liked or at least not disliked by cons with more clout. The

71

pickpocket's prestige enables him to run a small black-market operation in chocolates without getting hassled by screws or other cons. He's a small example of clout. For a big example you have to look at guys like Harold Rosale, Wallace Kearns, Phillip Valentine or John Hl.

You might be saying to yourself, "Oh, yes, those names are familiar." Before you muddy your mind with half-true, hazy remembrances, let me say you'll meet those four gentlemen later and you should try to keep your senses free of any memories so you can get a good impression from my introduction. OK? OK.

Those four dudes had real clout mainly because they had power on the Outside. A few other cons had influential external connections, too, but most of the important cons relied on the graces of one of those four big men. A lot of big guys who get nabbed on the Outside are surprised to find out just how little their external accomplishments count once the doors start shutting behind them.

To give you an example of just how important those four men were, let's talk about Wally (called that only with permission) Kearns' vacation to the Bahamas. Wally decided he needed a break from the pressures of prison, so he left his custom-redesigned four-cell suite with its color television, stereo–hi-fi rig, king-size bed, stove for warming up light snacks, refrigerator and three-line phone for two weeks of roughing it in the West Indies. He stayed at the warden's beach house, which the warden could afford only because of Mr. Kearns.

Now that's clout.

It's hard to say which of the Big Four was the most powerful before they expanded to become the Big Five and a Half. It would be easy to pick John Hl as having the least, since he never had enough to get out of Havensbrook for a rest. But then John Hl's was special.

What about that sixty percent chunk of cons who don't have clout? What about them? For them the rules and ins and outs of prison only mean one thing: Don't mess with any of the anointed. Other than that, the only rule for the clout-less cons is survival.

I was in the cloutless cons group.

When I first arrived at Havensbrook, I was in limbo. The prison grapevine hadn't yet evaluated my potential and/or power. I tried to prolong my nebulous state as long as possible. But the grapevine also discovered I wasn't on the best of terms with my leader and partner (Donnely did not tell them). When it became apparent that I didn't have any important connections with the Outside or my gang, it was only a matter of time. After I didn't make any overtures to the Powers That Be—not the screws, the cons with clout—I "joined" the cloutless mob.

My status was announced in a rather spectacular, though not unprecedented, fashion on a Tuesday morning three weeks after I entered Heaven. A big six-four goon in for Murder One performed on a New York policeman strolled up to me in the exercise yard and told me his shoes were dusty and I was to clean them off.

Right then I knew the Moment of Truth had come. In a society like Heaven's cloutless cloister, once you dust off someone's shoes you're doomed. Pretty soon you find yourself kissing them and it's a quick, short step to even worse things. Nobody had to tell me that. "No" doesn't really carry a lot of weight with most cretins like the big con, so I flexed my muscles as unobtrusively as I could, stepped back easily into a stance Raoul taught us in our self-defense training and told the mother he was full of shit.

That's when it hit the fan.

The gorilla had expected and I think even hoped for a refusal. That gave him an excuse, which he didn't need but liked. He swung his leg up in the classic attempt to deposit his foot in my groin. I easily parried his kick and countered with a backhand snap to his face. Unfortunately he was taller than I am and the distance was a little greater than I thought. I only bloodied his nose; I didn't break it. While he was still slightly surprised, I side-thrust kicked him in the stomach with everything I had. He grunted, doubled up and backed away. When my foot was planted firmly on the ground I hit his head with the edge of my right hand. I missed his temple, but I didn't break my hand and he went down.

73

By this time most of the other cons in the courtyard had gathered around us. A screw on the wall was watching, but it wasn't worth his while to interfere. He did call a buddy over to watch the fight.

My last vestiges of civilization pulled me up short of kicking my opponent in his head, a luxury I shouldn't have indulged in. He lay stunned for a second on the ground, then quickly rolled away. When he bounded up, he had a knife in his hand. He became the third most fear-inspiring man I have ever met, although at the time I had not yet met either the first- or second-place winners. I looked at Number 3's blood-smeared ugly face and his knife and swallowed. It wasn't one of those homemade hand-ground spoon-and-broomstick devices. It was a real, honest-to-goodness (if you'll pardon the expression), South Side of Chicago Hell's Kitchen Tijuana-made eight-inch switchblade.

I didn't have any more time to think about what real heaven would be like before the goon made the mistake of rushing me. He should have sparred with me, slicing off little chunks at a time, but he was so mad he waded in for a big butcher scene.

I blocked his right hand and knife with my left forearm. I still have a cute little scar. I pivoted counterclockwise, so his rush rammed his body into my right side; then immediately after contact I grabbed his groin with my right hand and squeezed with every muscle I could use. He yelled, doubled up slightly and pushed me away, causing himself even greater pain and putting him exactly where I wanted him. I twisted his right arm down and smashed his elbow with my fist. He dropped the knife. I heard the joint break and back-kicked to his ribs, breaking more bones. I kicked again and dislocated his knee. As he fell, I kicked a third time, smashing his face. He hit the ground then, so my fourth kick only bruised his kidneys.

Not very pretty, right? But that's what it's like when you don't have clout.

I stood panting, looking at the circle of cons and the lump of meat on the ground. I picked up the switchblade. It was

74

sharp enough to shave with. Prison custom and possible survival to avoid later revenge dictated that I should take that knife and push it between the hulk's ribs. The other cons stood around waiting, watching me to see what I would do.

I shut the knife, put it in my pocket and walked away. When I thought about the fight that night, I was sick.

After that some sort of word went out. The gist of it was I might not be a "wise guy" or a big man, but I was one mean mother. I was glad of that reputation since it saved me from doing something like the fight again and probably losing, because while the training Raoul and the Marines gave me was excellent and I was in shape from doing calisthenics for hours on end to forget where I was, my heart wasn't in that kind of survival technique. My head made me keep the knife.

After the fight some of the younger cloutless cons, two kids originally busted for draft resistance and a couple busted for marijuana raps, began to pal around with me, partially because they thought I might be developing clout and partially because we liked each other.

The con in the fight? It seems I wasn't his only enemy. Somebody injected him with an overdose of morphine while he was recovering in the prison hospital.

I've lost a lot of sleep wondering who was really to blame for the pebble in his pond.

On the forty-eighth day I was in prison I had 10,902 days left to serve. I also had a letter. Now my folks were dead, none of my other relatives knew where I was, and the only friends I had who would write me were in The Group. Of course, all my correspondents besides my attorney had to get permission to write from the authorities. I knew the Professor could get me any correspondent. He was clout. I really wanted to hear from Meredith, but I didn't request that. All my correspondence excepting that from my attorney was censored. I sat looking at the censor-opened envelope for a long time that morning before I opened it. I wanted to prolong the sensation of having a letter from the Outside as long as possible.

I knew right away the letter was a fake. For one thing it was in Larry's handwriting; for another it was from my cousin Paul. I don't have any cousin Paul. I read the letter anyway.

Dear Cousin Jack,

It is painful for me to write to you, partially because I wish you were here so much and I can only sympathize with you and hope you are well and everything is fine. Everything is fine here too. The business Mr. Franklin [our code name for Alfred] and I are working for is going well, all according to plan, or so says the boss. I guess we just have to have faith in him since he hasn't slipped up yet. I think your pet chameleon [code name for Reginald] really misses you, because his changes have lacked luster lately, although he is doing a fine job for a chameleon. That cute little Puerto Rican boy next door [Raoul? I thought] is going to school [working with the Professor?]. I hear he is getting good marks. Oh, remember the old man down the block, Herbie Daniels [Meredith's code name. Meredith!]? Well, he says for you to take good care of yourself and to tell your friend [Donnely, of course] to be very sure to do the same.

Well, I can't think of anything else to say. When you find time, drop me a note to let me know if there's anything new with you or anything I can do. I sincerely remain,

Your cousin,
Paul

The letter bothered me for a number of different reasons. For example, Larry kept implying that everything was going according to plan. The Plan? Going well? With me—and, of course, Donnely—in prison? That really bothered me, but it made me think. It sounded as if The Group were still together. Were they working on a way to get us out? Larry didn't say or even hint.

I was also bothered by Meredith's addition. It didn't do much to bolster my spirits. A small request for me to take care of myself and a strong injunction for Donnely to do the same. It was easy to see what she meant by that.

I spent the rest of the day brooding.

After dinner one of the screws came and rattled the bars on my cage. "Hey, Mason, look alive. We finally got you a roomie."

I swung to a sitting position on my bunk. This could be one of three things or shades of all of them: good, indifferent or bad. Whatever it was, I probably wouldn't know right away since it would take time to get to know the dude. Oh, well, I thought, I've got lots of time.

I was wrong about not knowing how it would be, thinking it would take me awhile to decide. I knew right away, the minute my new roomie stepped into the cell. It was very, very good.

My new roomy was Daniel James Donnely and I was at long last going to get to kill the mother.

The Plan

One thing you had to say for John Hl: If he hated you only a little, he wasn't such a repulsive, fear-inspiring guy. You could almost consider tolerating him like a normal human being.

John Hl hated me only a little, or at least during this stage of The Plan he hated me only a little. He really hated everyone. That's what the "H" stood for. He payed me the supreme outsiders' compliment the day he measured me for my "graduation suit." John Hl has had a lot of practice measuring people for suits since he used to work in a Detroit funeral parlor as a fitter and dresser while he was an apprentice mortician. Of course, when he was taking care of dead bodies, he hadn't yet "seen the burnin' blazin' light of the cold naked truth." After his revelation, he started making dead bodies for other people to measure. What John Hl told me as he fitted me in the prison tailor shop was, "Mason, you slimy motherfucker, you almost got some of it together."

I was deeply touched. John Hl's compliment didn't exactly mean I'm an OK Mother Brother, let alone a Righteous Right On, but at least it meant I was not a bad dude. I thanked him as warmly as I could in a way he would understand. I saluted him with my middle finger.

Both John H1 and his drum brother John H9 warmly responded with the same gesture.

I suppose you are wondering what happened in the approximately five months between the screw bringing Donnely to my cell and John H1 fitting me for what the cons call a graduation suit. I suppose I better tell you, too, because that time period makes up the guts of Phase II.

I sat on my bunk, gathering my legs beneath me and waiting for the screw to leave. I didn't say a word. I flexed my muscles as unobtrusively as I could. While the screw was manually locking the door, Donnely put his stuff on his bed. I watched him. While the screw's footsteps were fading down the iron hall, Donnely stood by his bunk looking at me. I looked back. When the screw slammed the iron corridor door behind him, I rushed Donnely.

The next few seconds aren't very clear in my mind. I know Donnely got off an incredibly fast side-snap kick which thumped me in my stomach, but after that things are kind of hazy. I remember flying through the air. My next coherent memory is of me face down on my bunk, Donnely's knee in my back and my right arm locked in a very effective hold. I couldn't move an inch without hurting myself.

Donnely told me later that he and Raoul had practiced for a year before I even started training with The Group.

Donnely spoke as I fought to regain my breath. "Now, Jack, Jack, calm down. I know you're mad and I know you've got a right to be, but it's not like you think it is."

I tried to say "you son of a bitch," but Donnely pressed his knee down just a little. He later said he hadn't wanted me to waste my effort on ill-considered words.

"Jack, the one thing you always agreed was that I was honest. I still think you know I am and know that I would not lie to you. Keep that in mind.

"You're upset because you're in prison. Well, I don't blame you. But remember, you agreed with me about the concept of short-term temporary sacrifice and long-term investment, right?" He didn't let me answer before he continued. "Right. So think, think about what I'm going to tell you.

"Everything is going according to The Plan. Everything is all right. Remember the letter you got this morning? I know you got one, but I can only guess what's in it. I'm sure they said everything is going according to plan. They did, didn't they?"

He eased up on the pressure and I slowly, grudgingly, nodded yes.

"Good. Now, Jack, in a few seconds I'm going to let you get

up so I can talk with you better. I don't want you to attack me again and have to go through all this. I'd just have to hurt you some more and I don't want to do that. You're my best friend. Besides, it would upset The Plan and everybody would be in trouble. I'm sure you don't want that. But I'll tell you what I'll do, I'll promise you this. I'll let you up and talk with you about what's going on. If you still feel like killing me afterward, I'll let you get the knife and try again. If you have a blade, it should almost be a fair fight. OK?"

What choice did I have? I nodded yes.

He sat on his bunk and waited until my breath came back. Then he started.

"As you know, the bank job went exactly according to The Plan. And I mean exactly. Now I know this is kind of hard for you to understand when you first hear it, but it was part of The Plan that we go to prison."

"But why?" I interrupted. "Why? How can we have succeeded if we're in prison for another twenty-nine-plus years? You can't call that 'long-term gain'!"

Donnely smiled and held up his hand to make me quiet down. "Think, Jack, think. The reason for The Plan is to take care of us, all of us in The Group, to provide us with security so we would be OK for the rest of our lives. Right?"

"Right!" I yelled, ignoring his gesture. "We stole the money so we could have it because it would buy us the security we wanted."

"And there's the flaw!" exclaimed Donnely, pouncing on my statement like the Professor pouncing on an opposing attorney who can't quote the federal code. "There's the fundamental flaw with every criminal operation. For, even if we do succeed in the job initially, there's always the possibility of a postoperative slipup, something that will go wrong, maybe way in the future, so our security will be jeopardized and we may go to prison."

"But we're in prison now!" I wailed.

"Precisely!" exclaimed Donnely excitedly. "Therefore, The Plan has obviously succeeded! We don't have to worry about making a mistake and going to prison in the future because we're already there!"

I put my head in my hands for a long time. When I raised it to look at Donnely's grinning face, all my anger toward him was gone. "Donnely," I said, "as your best friend let me tell you something. You've slipped a few gears upstairs; you've flipped."

"Stay with me for a while, Jack, trust me. You see, not only are we safe, but the rest of The Group is, too, at least unless they goof. The authorities have their bank robbers.

"Now I don't want to be a martyr either. I don't intend to spend the rest of my life here. Why, for one thing, I'll be through with all the books in the prison library that I haven't read in a few months. Of course, there are other reasons why I want to get out, too."

Like Meredith, I thought painfully.

"So now look at our problem. We have to get out of prison and we have to do so in such a way that we are secure and The Group is secure, not just temporarily, but permanently. And we have to do so while maintaining the same goals we started with when we hit the bank. Right?"

I shrugged. My mind was too tired to care.

"Right. But there's more to it than that. You see, Jack, the bank robbery and us going to prison, this particular prison I might add, are only part of The Plan."

My mind woke up a little. My mouth said, "What?"

"That's right, only part. Just like our advertising campaign in California. Remember? Preliminaries. One thing leads naturally to another. Everything flows."

"But if we didn't rob a bank to rob the bank, why did we rob the bank?"

"Because it's part of The Plan."

Right then I almost hit him, or at least I almost tried again. Instead I said, "Tell me."

He did.

I had to admit it made some kind of sense.

I also agreed to continue with The Plan. What other choice did I have?

I also let him read Larry's letter. I figured more of it was for him than for me.

We started the next day. Actually, Donnely had started

81

long before we hit prison, but *we* didn't start until he came to me, obviously. Donnely had spent a month and about twenty thousand dollars buying influence. He now had enough to be called at least a medium power, which partially explains how he had been able to keep me from having a cellmate until he was ready to move in. He apologized for failing to prevent the incident in the yard, but he told me that was why he had made sure I had a lot of unarmed combat experience and training. He also said that my rep as a tough fighter hadn't hurt him, my partner, in building even more clout.

I was nervous all the next morning, for Donnely had told me what the first stage of the operation was right after he explained to me why he hadn't told me about the necessity of our prison session before we pulled the bank job.

"Look at it this way," Donnely explained. "If you had known you had to go to prison, you might not have put your whole heart into the operation. That would have damaged your expertise and, eventually, endangered The Plan and The Group. So I didn't tell you. The rest of The Group didn't find out until they reached the rendezvous point. The Professor knew and he had quite a time keeping them from chucking everything and coming to rescue you."

I looked at Donnely and said, "OK, I understand. Now let me ask you a question. Are you going to tell me everything about The Plan from now on, complete with the details of my role?"

Donnely frowned. "Look at it this way, Jack. I will try never to lie to you, nor will I do anything which, in the long run, is not to your benefit. Do you still want to ask your question, knowing that my answer may make you more nervous than you already are, thus increasing the odds that you will make a mistake, botch The Plan, endanger The Group and put you here or worse for the rest of your life?"

I withdrew my question.

Then he told me about the first stage of the operation.

The reason I was so nervous the next morning was the meeting scheduled for that afternoon. All the cons and screws considered it a miracle that Donnely had been able to

organize the meeting at all. If he could pull it off and
live . . . well, that would be an even bigger miracle. For you
see, we were meeting that afternoon with Harold Rosale,
Wallace Kearns, Phillip Valentine and John Hl.

Oh, you say.

Now not that there was any animosity or hostility in the
group, with the natural exception of John H1's universal
hate. Rosale, Kearns and Valentine had been known to nod
and even speak to each other. Politely. It was just that there is
absolutely no trust or love in their kind of world outside the
pen and there, on the inside, where strange things have been
known to happen, they regarded each other like hungry
lions in a pride where meat might suddenly become scarce.
Daniel James Donnely and I were going to walk into that
lions' den with nobody but ourselves to seal shut their jaws.

For those of you who don't remember all the details of
their illustrious lives, I will briefly introduce those four gentlemen. I hope that if they or their associates read this, they
will remember me with the warm kindness they are so capa-
ble of. In order of incarceration we have:

Harold Rosale. Harold Rosale should never have been in
prison by all that's right and holy and American, or so he
says. If he had been born prior to Teddy Roosevelt, it might
have been his grandson who was governor of New York. Unfortunately, Harold was born during the era of Franklin
Roosevelt. By the time Harold was old enough to take over
the family's multimillion-dollar holdings most of the business
practices he enjoys employing were illegal. Harold likes to
think of himself as a victim of creeping socialism and a pinko
government lab technician who refused an "honorarium"
and said one of Harold's products was unsafe for human or
animal use. The lab technician reported the bribe to his su-
perior, who had accepted one of Harold's bribes. The matter
should have ended there. Unfortunately for Harold, the
technician turned out to be one of those persistent fools who
mind other people's business. The technician wrote to a
Senator who is a member of the party Harold doesn't like.
The Senator immediately instituted an investigation which

83

resulted in, among other things, Harold's being convicted of thirty-two counts of bribery, extortion, price-fixing, fraud and similar time-tested business activities. Harold was sentenced to ten years, the minimum possible sentence. (The Professor refused his case.) The lab technician lost his job and could find work only as a dishwasher. The Senator lost his next election to a semiretarded ex-football player with a great smile and ten million dollars in campaign donations from various sources.

Wallace Kearns. If Harold Rosale should never have been in prison, Wallace Kearns most definitely should have been, by his own admission. Mr. Kearns started out as a humble Jewish immigrant trying to make a buck in the post-World War II days. He joined a progressive industry and soon became a well-respected businessman, community leader and head of a large household. Mr. Kearns eventually became a vice-president, a position he held in absentia while resting in Havensbrook. At the same time Mr. Kearns was making his way in the business world, a tough, somewhat homicidal hoodlum nicknamed Wild Wally (later, Mr. W.) was ice-picking, machine-gunning and bombing his way up the chain of command of what is called, among other things, the Syndicate. Eventually, after several large funerals, the board members of the Syndicate decided it was easier and more profitable (Wally has excellent business sense) to promote Wally to vice-president than to eliminate him. And so they did. Perhaps you are not surprised to learn that Wild Wally the Hoodlum and Mr. Kearns the Respected Businessman are one and the same. Wally entered Havensbrook by choice. A few of his past exploits were catching up with him—namely, some vindictive relatives of his deceased competitors. The trouble was being taken care of, but the best prognosticators on Wally's staff thought it might take as long as a year to root out all the troublesome areas. Wally, for safety's sake, retreated to the comfort of Havensbrook after turning himself in for a minor tax offense.

Phillip Valentine. Phil, as everyone is ordered to call him, is another self-made man of whom we can all be proud. Phil

84

started organizing workers along the docks of San Francisco in the late thirties. He was the oldest of the four leaders we were going to meet and the toughest, at least physically. Phil eventually left the docks for the heartland of America. There he organized the forty-four-thousand-member United Laborers and Workers Union from scratch and the remnants of the unions which had been flourishing until Phil arrived on the scene. Phil had a very effecive organizing slogan: "You will join." As the record shows, he was tremendously successful. Phil came to Havensbrook after a scab-riddled white-collar jury found him guilty of stealing two million dollars from his union's strike and retirement funds. In a special election conducted and supervised by Phil's handpicked officers the union members overwhelmingly endorsed a statement saying they didn't care if good old Phil stole from them or not. Unfortunately, the results of this election did not sway the jury, which goes to show you in how much trouble American democracy is. Something, however, swayed the judge and Phil only pulled a two-year sentence out of a possible twenty.

Last but not least is John H1. John H1's ancestors were slaves imported from Africa, but John H1's heritage means nothing to him. John H1 was the founder and at that time the leader of the Spiritual and Revolutionary Brotherhood of the Tom Toms, an organization which the New York *Times* wrongly labeled a radical militant black political terrorist group. The three white Tom Toms in San Quentin left the Aryan Brotherhood for the Tom Toms, "to be where the action was!" There are about one hundred Tom Toms. What all Tom Toms have in common is their hatred for everyone and everything. I can't really tell you what they stand for, because except for the hate thing nobody, not even—I think—John H1 knows. The best description I found of the Tom Toms was in a Chicago *Daily News* column. The writer said the Tom Toms "combine the worst elements of the Hell's Angels, the Ku Klux Klan, the Waffen SS and the Jesus Freaks." I have heard John H1 call Malcolm X, Eldridge Cleaver and Huey Newton "flaming gutless Uncle Toms." John H1 told me the Black Panthers, the Deacons for De-

fense and the Black Muslims were "whitewashed liberal ene-
my sellouts." Once the "head drum" casually labeled Guy
Fawkes, John Brown and John Dillinger as "flippant." John
H1 told Donnely the only historical figures he has any
friendly feelings toward are the Marquis de Sade, Adolf Hit-
ler, Joseph Stalin, Rasputin and Attila the Hun (whom,
Donnely claims, John H1 doesn't understand). What the
Tom Toms do is simple: almost whatever they want to and
aren't stopped from. Which of course is why John H1 was in
Havensbrook. Last year he gave the occupants of 1600 Penn-
sylvania Avenue, Washington, D.C., thirty minutes to clear
out so he could use their house for an office. He came back to
enforce his eviction with a shotgun and three drum brothers.
The "fascist-communist-reactionary-pseudo kangaroo court"
found his real estate claim invalid and allotted him and his
surviving companion, drum brother John H9, cells in Havensbrook. If you think that you now don't have to worry
about the Tom Toms, think again. John H1 still has a few
drum brothers walking around the country, hating and waiting orders or opportunity.

These were the friendly people Donnely and I were going
to meet with that day. Representatives of four major pillars
of American society: big business, organized crime, professional labor and fanaticism. Each one of them had clout, both
inside and outside the prison.

For The Plan, Donnely needed that clout.

We held the meeting in the chaplain's study. The warden
would have let us use his office and conference room, but he
was afraid of getting bloodstains on the carpet. He would
have let us anyway, but nobody wanted to push the point. To
show his gratitude for our understanding consideration, he
sent two bottles of his best cognac to the meeting room.

Donnely, Harold Rosale, Wallace Kearns and Phillip ("Call
me Phil") Valentine sat around a table sipping cognac and
exchanging mild pleasantries. John H1 sat in the far corner,
scowling and hating everything. He refused the cognac because it might be poisoned. I sat by Donnely. Tough, leathery Phil Valentine sat to Donnely's left. Dapper Harold Ro-

sale sat across from Donnely. Wallace Kearns, looking like a mild pensioner, sat across from me, nodding and smiling. To my immediate right and his left sat Bruno, his six-eight bodyguard, looking like a Sherman tank complete with weaponry. (You should remember Bruno for later. I never forget him.) I turned away from that unpleasant sight and my eyes fell on John H9 with his three-foot bolo knife standing guard by his leader. That didn't comfort me in the least.

I didn't feel very good.

"Well, gentlemen," Donnely said, gently setting his empty cognac glass on the table, "there's an old line which goes, 'I suppose you're wondering why I called you here today.' I think that line is appropriate at this time. In addition to that, I suppose you are wondering why I chose to enter this prison."

Donnely's bomb got the reaction he planned. Rosale grimaced, John H1 snorted, and Phil Valentine laughed out loud. Wallace Kearns merely frowned and that bothered me.

"You trying to tell us you *planned* to be here?" Labor leader Phil's voice was far from friendly.

"Precisely," replied Donnely. "I—with the help of my associates—held up that bank and I turned myself in—with my colleague Mr. Mason—partially in order that I might enter this prison."

"May I ask why, Mr. Donnely?" inquired Kearns of the Syndicate.

Donnely smiled. "So I might meet with you gentlemen today."

That was some more of Donnely's strange explanation and reasoning, at least I thought so, but Kearns frowned and said, "Continue, if you will, Mr. Donnely, you're making sense."

Donnely smiled and continued. "As you gentlemen know, my Group realized about three-quarters of a million dollars in profit from our Hamilton banking enterprise. That money has since been deposited in numerous other banks, withdrawn and reassembled in the First State Citizens' Bank of Hamilton, Arizona, under my Group's legitimate control.

"I intend to use that laundered money combined with funds and services you gentlemen control through one means or another to legitimately quadruple my capital. I intend to do so in a relatively short period of time, say, three to five months. Your funds will experience the same growth ratio as mine. When I have reached my desired profit level, I shall pull out of our mutual consortium and sever all our connections. I am sure you will find the arrangement profitable, enjoyable and more than satisfactory."

Nobody grimaced. Harold Rosale, Wall Street's representative, spoke first. "How exactly do you expect to acquire this massive financial gain, and what role do we four play in your . . . shall we call it *fanciful* scheme?"

Donnely smiled. "I prefer to call it *imaginative,* Mr. Rosale, but each to his own adjectives. Let me explain.

"You four gentlemen possess varying degrees of wealth, power, knowledge and what we shall call connections. I propose to blend your resources with my imagination and my Group's efforts and resources in such a manner that we can realize our profits."

Kearns stirred slightly in his chair. "These general statements are all very nice and no doubt very true, but I cannot consider them as having much value without some specific examples—hypothetical if you wish—to back them up. Give me three."

Donnely did. When he was finished, the room was quiet for some time. Even John H1 stopped his mutterings.

"Suppose," Harold Rosale said at last, "suppose we agree. What will it cost us?"

Donnely smiled. He was halfway home. "One million clean dollars each, with the exception of Mr. H1 and his organization, who do not have such a sum at their disposal, plus your assistance in organizing and managing the endeavors as I direct them."

"What do we get in return?" demanded friendly Phil.

"I have already mentioned the figure of a quadrupled gain," said Donnely. "In other words, three million additional clean dollars. Since Mr. H1 and his associates are not investing cash, I suggest they receive a flat one million out of the expense money. I also intend to have a good deal of fun, if that appeals to you."

Phil snorted.

"What kind of guarantee do we have that you will succeed, Mr. Donnely?" Kearns' voice was soft, his words easy and his face *the* most frightening I have ever seen. I wanted back in the yard with shiv-toting, cloutless goons.

Donnely didn't flinch. He looked straight at Kearns and said, "I should think that is obvious."

Mr. Kearns smiled his face back to normal. "I hope it is," he said.

Nobody had to tell me what the penalty for failure was.

Kearns had another question. "Supposing once the consortium is successful, we, the major backers, do not wish to disassociate ourselves from you and your associates. We might wish to continue such a profitable enterprise."

Donnely smiled. "That would be foolish. For one thing, the activities we will be mounting will be of such a scale that they will eventually attract a good deal of attention. When that happens, the work involved in making them a success rapidly reduces the profit margin to a meaningless pitance. The consortium then becomes a liability for each of us. Another reason is that I do not work under coercive pressure; I merely function. My Group operates in the same fashion. There would be no profit in forcing an association."

We had another long silence; then Mr. Kearns glanced at Mr. Rosale, who nodded. Kearns glanced at Phil Valentine, who merely shrugged. From the corner came a sarcastic but affirmative grunt. Kearns, who had obviously been chosen as spokesman for our colleagues, said, "I would like to make a speech.

"Mr. Donnely, Mr. Mason, I studied your bank job with great care and found it to be the best endeavor of its kind I have ever seen. A stroke of creative genius from beginning right up to the end. At the end I was initially disappointed. Now I find the genius has carried through, at least as far as this room and today's meeting. I see no reason to nip genius in the bud. I accept your conditions, join your operation and wish you well. For both our sakes, I hope you succeed."

Kearns leaned back in his chair, as peacefully relaxed as if he had just finished a feast in his own home. Donnely bowed slightly in his direction.

"I agree," interjected Harold Rosale, "and you can be sure I shall participate fully."

"Well," said Phil, "me and the boys have gambled before for the good of the workingman. I figure once more won't hurt. The United Laborers and Workers Union votes to participate in this here endeavor."

From the corner came John H1's booming voice. "Fascist-communist exploitive pigs, the Spiritual and Revolutionary Brotherhood of the Tom Toms, in its infinite wisdom, has seen fit to join with you in this temporary transitory alliance and at least the Brotherhood will keep its word, despite the trail of broken promises and maligned dreams left by others. Let it be known that we, the wave of the future and the nightmares of the past, will not shirk in our holy quest for. . . ."

The rest of us left before John H1 finished his sermon and acceptance speech.

Figure it out for yourselves. Donnely had just promised four of the most dangerous and powerful men anyone could ever meet that he would take half a million of his own money and three million of theirs and, in approximately five months, turn that already sizable kitty into at least fourteen million dollars after expenses (which included John H1's million). All while incarcerated in a federal prison.

Sure, you bet your life, you say sarcastically. Which was, of course, what he had done. I think it was implicit that mine was wagered also.

Of course he did it, for if he hadn't, I wouldn't be sitting here writing this. I didn't actually "see" most of the action, but The Group have all told me stories which illustrate this phase of The Plan. I'll tell you a few of their stories as examples of The Plan in action.

Example 1. The fat figure in the black swivel chair looked as if it belonged in a reptilian specimen jar instead of behind an

90

executive desk, but the name Thomas Wise belonged on both the creature's driver's license and the door to the executive suite.

The attorney visiting Wise noticed a strange glaze in Wise's pinkish eyes, an exhausted glaze of bewilderment and perhaps worry, but a glaze that still showed *something* in control. The attorney had known a somewhat different Wise years before. Wise had always been physically and mentally obscene, but he had been almost lackadaisical, never showing stress, indeed, seldom showing any feelings save anger, lust or satisfaction. The two men had worked together on numerous projects before Wise's greed induced him to ask the attorney to perform tasks the attorney found repugnant. Unlike many diplomaed guardians of justice, the attorney severed his relationship with his client rather than slice through his own ethics. The two men parted civilly. They had never actually liked each other. Theirs had been a purely "professional" relationship.

Now the two former business associates were reunited. On an ordinary day such an occurrence would have alerted the vast reservoir of base instincts Wise used in place of intellect, but that day was no ordinary day. The attorney even thought that Wise found some relief in his presence, some solace from the return of a familiar and nonantagonistic face. The attorney hoped his assessment was valid as he watched a strange gleam flicker through Wise's eyes during their discussion. The lawyer wondered about that gleam and about the muted wailing sounds coming from somewhere behind the closed ornate double doors.

Pudgy little boy Tommy Wise, neighborhood sneak, grew into obese Thomas Wise, corporate king who still perspired profusely despite his position as president of the massive conglomerate Jamex, Ltd. Tommy pushed his chunky right forefinger past his thick lips to tap on his green teeth for a moment's reflection before he resumed light conversation with his visitor. Tommy's left hand made a pudgy little fist around a small vial. That fist shook slightly, rattling the contents of the vial to a peculiar rhythm.

"It is good to see you, Bart," Tommy said lightly. "The only good thing about today as a matter of fact. I was curious when I heard you retired to some godforsaken place."

"Forsaken places abound," replied the counselor cryptically but tactfully, "and it's more a narrowing of my activities rather than a full-fledged retirement. I only handle a few clients these days. I like the freedom I have to visit old acquaintances and keep up with events. I spend most of my working time as a . . . well, a facilitator rather than an attorney. The law itself is not so exciting as it once was.

"But tell me, things don't sound very good for you. Which is strange. After all, Jamex lists on Wall Street at—what is it? Seventy-five?"

"Actually it's eighty-one and a half or at least it was when the board opened this morning," replied Tommy as he withdrew his finger from his mouth. A trickle of saliva ran from his finger to his dark-blue suit. He didn't seem to notice. "But that won't last long. I'll be lucky if it closes today at fifty."

"What makes you say that?"

Tommy's childhood acquaintances—he had no friends—called him Tommy the Toad. The corporate king heaved his massive, shuddering bulk to its feet and waddled to the picture window overlooking Fifth Avenue. The Toad had never been a hopper. He waved one short, fleshy forepaw. "Come over here and look at this."

Tommy's former attorney did as he was beckoned. He peered down to the street thirty stories below. "What is it? All I see is people, traffic, nothing unus— Wait a minute. Are those three old cars parked in front of the building across the street what you wanted me to see?" His host nodded and the attorney continued, "Well, what about them? What are they?"

"I'll tell you one thing for sure," snorted Tommy as he waddled back to his massive padded chair, panting slightly as he exerted himself. "They ain't no goddamn picket line. In the old days you at least had the picket lines. You could deal with them. Bust 'em up or let 'em walk their fool feet off. There were so many of them that after a while nobody even read their signs. But I've never seen anything like this. They just sit there in those old jalopies, waiting. Spooky. When the word gets out, Jamex will take a plunge like you've never seen."

"Who are they?" asked the attorney as he returned to his chair.

"They call themselves the Tom Toms." Tommy sighed. "At first I thought they were making fun of me, you know, a practical joke like those pie-in-the-face guys. But they ain't joking. I did some checking on them and they're a for-real group. This morning they marched into the outer office and announced that they were investigating Jamex's social policies, and if they didn't like them, they were going to take action. That's what they said, 'action.' Then they marched out. They've been sitting in those old cars ever since. They're parked in front of the hydrant, right where I normally have Clive park my limo, but no cop seems to want to stop and give them a ticket, even though I called to let the precinct know they weren't covered in the pad.

"My people tell me they're supposed to be pretty tough cookies, if you know what I mean. So I figured it's a little shakedown. That I don't mind, as long as it's in reason and we can write it off as a business expense. I sent my secretary Jergens down with five grand from petty cash and a message that we'd kick in some more to their Christmas kids' party or whatever the hell it is this batch uses for a screen. Jergens came back up and says they took the money but didn't say a thing. After half an hour they're still sitting there. I figure maybe they're serious about something, maybe more of that equality crap.

"I sent down Martha, you know, that cute little colored chick we put through Vassar under the write-off scholarship program you helped us draw up. She's doing pretty good, all things considered. Some of my people even want to start giving her stuff besides the kind of PR we use her for, but I say she ain't really up to that kind of thing. I mean, you know, she's got her place and her job and why pull the poor kid in over her head? Anyways, I sent Martha, figuring if nothing else those guys would like her tight little ass and that will calm them down so they'll work with our civil rights flack people.

"No dice. Ten minutes later Martha bursts into the office, screaming and hollering. She's been crying and carrying on all morning. Had to shut her up in the boardroom with two girls from steno. They still haven't calmed her down and I still don't know what went on out there.

"Just before lunch I figure, OK, these punks want to mess around. I'll quit being Mr. Nice Guy and Mr. Fair Deal.

"I got these guys, see, a dozen of them. Used to play pro ball. They do odd jobs for me. I sent them down to have a little talk with these Tom Toms; then I went over to the window to watch the fun. My guys and the Tom Toms walk down the alley to have their discussion. Just before Gladys brings me my before-lunch pick-me-up, a whole mess of them punks march back out of the alley, flip the bird up to the window like they know I'm watching, then get back in their cars and start sitting again. I've quit going to the window to look for my boys. Jergens says he'll resign before he goes down there to find them. So there those crazies sit and here I sit."

"You do have a problem," noted the lawyer, "but you've handled things like this before."

"Yeah, but usually I've got time to move, I can devote myself to the little things. But today. . . . You ain't heard the half of it!"

"There's more?"

"Listen," continued his host, leaning as far forward as his stomach would allow, "I'm downing my martini and thinking about what I'm going to have for lunch, putting those crazies out of my mind until later, and in walks the head foreman from our main plant. It seems the United Laborers and Workers are unhappy with what they're getting from Jamex, which doesn't make sense, because I pay those labor officers plenty out of petty cash. *Plenty.* They're talking about a general strike. If they go out, *everybody* goes out, no question about that."

94

"My, that does sound bad."

"Put me right off my lunch, if you can imagine that. Right off." Tommy shook his rattling left hand vigorously to emphasize his point. "About the time I'm beginning to get my nerves under control again, my sales manager staggers in. He's crying. Rosale Industries, our biggest customer ever, called him to cancel their orders. He barely gets the words out before hysteria sets in. Christ, I had to put him in the boardroom with poor Martha. They're in there now, bawling and screaming their heads off like a couple of babies."

Tommy paused for a second to take a sip from the martini pitcher. He leaned forward to confide in his ex-associate. "I tell you true," Tommy muttered lowly, "the only reason I'm not in there with them is the little red ones."

"The little red ones?" ventured his guest.

"Yeah, the little red ones." The corporate mogul's meaty paw trembled only slightly as he pushed the almost-empty prescription bottle across the desk. His eyes stared at the opaque plastic vial while his mouth released his secrets. "They're really great. Keep you wide awake but really calm, really cool. I mean, I know my ass is in the sling. My whole company is crumbling under me, right? My whole life is about to fall right down, everything. My job and the one hundred thousand shares of solid little blue-chip Jamex stock I sunk my savings into so I could get control of the company; my season tickets to the Jets with the special Super Bowl clause; my purebred Great Dane, my wife, Emma, and her split-level in Scarsdale; the two—no, it's three kids; that blond whore I keep stashed on Central Park West; everything, just waiting to crumble into dust.

"Now most men would be disturbed by all this to say the least. Panicky would be a better word. Screaming bejesus, like Martha and my sales manager. But not me. I'm slightly alarmed, but cool, calm, in command. All thanks to these great little red ones. They kind of pull and push you even and tight, then string you along with whatever happens. It's kind of fun, like watching a movie. It's almost entertaining to see all this happen. I had a hell of a time after you left me until I found out about the little red ones. Now everything just flows."

"What will you do when you run out of little red ones or when they wear off?"

"I'll probably kill myself," replied Tommy calmly as he shifted his head to watch the light as it passed through the plastic bottle. "I think I'll jump out the window, like Grampa did. I hope I splat and spoil all the upholstery on those goddamn jalopies too." His voice rose slightly toward the end of his outburst and his hand shook even more as he pointed to the window. But within seconds the little red ones brought concerned control back into his life and he once more smiled at his guest.

"Actually things wouldn't be too bad if I could find a way to pull my assets out of Jamex. I mean, so the company folds. So all those people lose jobs. Big deal. I can make it with my Swiss accounts. I'll have to give up either Emma and the dog or the whore, but what the hell, times are tough and we all have to make sacrifices. If I could figure out a way to unload what I've got without taking a big hosing, I'd be happy. But if I try and dump my stocks in time, I'll get caught. You know it's illegal for me to use inside private information for personal gain in the company I own and work for. There's nobody I know of who can handle all the complexities of this, plus come up with the money in time. . . ."

The attorney tried not to smile as he watched Tommy's eyes shift from the plastic bottle, their gleam burning with a bright new flame. "Say," began Tommy in what he thought was a nontransparent tone, "you said you've still got some connections, you don't suppose. . . ."

"That I could find a way and a body to take your stock off your hands? That would be a pretty tall order, Tommy."

"But you can do it," Tommy said eagerly before the little red ones pulled his excitement back down. "You, if anybody. You know the law and you've got the connections!"

Tommy's voice dropped as he muttered, "I'd make it well worth your while."

The attorney frowned at Tommy's last offer as if a sour

96

note had been struck during a concert. "I'm not your associate," he remonstrated mildly but firmly. He paused while the little red ones let Tommy feel some emotion. The attorney made a show of reconsidering, then let Tommy listen as he thought out loud.

"You can't profit from your inside knowledge and get away with it, that's true, but there's no law saying how much you have to lose. As I recall, you bought the stock at sixty-one several years ago. It's now at eighty-one. You say it will drop to fifty, but we both know that will only be the initial plunge. I'm betting that before you can unload all your shares, Jamex will be selling at around ten, if it is selling at all.

"What you could do is this: Sell your stocks now, in bulk, at a price far below today's quotation, say, twenty to thirty. You'll lose, but not so much that it will be disastrous. You'll be able to claim a tax loss, you will still have your job, and the law will be placated."

"I don't know if I like that," replied Tommy thoughtfully. "What if things pick up after the initial slump? Then where am I?"

The attorney snapped his fingers. He normally did not use that gesture, but he felt it would help bring Tommy and the little red ones to full attention. "I've got it. I have some clients, a new investment consortium called Charon. They're looking for property which will net them either a huge profit or a great tax write-off. They've got the cash and could move on this today. I can make this suggestion to them without jeopardizing my allegiance to their needs and still help you. You sell them your stock at, say, twenty. They guarantee that if at any time the stock recovers and goes back up to, say one hundred, you can buy it back. Let's make that binding, you have to buy it back, so if it goes any higher, it's guaranteed you won't have to pay more to get your control back. That way you're hedged on both ends, they make their profit or loss, and everybody is happy."

Tommy frowned. "I don't really like it. I lose money no matter what happens."

"But you know your losses, and you don't lose everything.

97

It's absolutely the best I can do for you," replied the attorney, his conscience for an ex-client salved to its necessary level.

Tommy's jowls quivered to a smile. "I'll do it! I'll do it! When can it happen? When can we sign the papers?"

The attorney smiled. "Right after I call and check with my clients at Charon. If you have your secretary come in here, I can dictate the necessary papers, your stenos can type them up, and since I have power of attorney for Charon, we can finalize everything within a couple of hours.

"You realize," emphasized the attorney softly, "this contract is binding. If the price does climb to the stated level, you *will* buy the stocks back immediately. Otherwise, Charon will take all you own and your dog, too."

"Oh, sure, I know," replied Tommy, his mind gleeful at the prospects of pulling a coup out of his tribulations.

The lawyer made his call. It took the steno pool two hours to type up the contracts. During that time the lawyer became aware of a growing din in the outer office, but he said nothing to Tommy. The attorney had insisted no one be allowed in to see the corporate king until after he left, and Tommy's secretary was enforcing that edict. Tommy didn't seem to care. As soon as the attorney had received the OK from his Charon clients, the Toad gleefully settled himself in his padded swivel chair to await the signing ceremony. While he waited he amused himself with the latest edition of *Fabulous Fannies*. The attorney stood at the window, watching traffic move down Fifth Avenue just as it does every Tuesday.

The ink was barely dry on the documents before Tommy bid his ex-lawyer a fond adieu. The attorney heard his former client use one hand to punch the phone buttons for a Central Park West number as Jergens, the Secretary, led the lawyer through the buffer hall leading to the outer office. Tommy's other hand flicked the pill vial, whirling it back and forth across his desktop. A smile grew on the attorney's face as he walked through the outer office, threading his way among the hordes of excited junior executives crowded around the reception desk. Amid their babble he discerned a few strains of interesting conversation:

98

—"*and not only did the union say they were mistaken about their complaints, they promised no labor problems for the next five years! Wait till the boss hears that!*"

—"*so when the big tough guy strolls in, we naturally thought we had had it, but he hands the receptionist this letter which says the Spiritual and Revolutionary Brotherhood of Tom Toms has found Jamex praiseworthy and vows to protect us from any misguided militants or crooks who think different!*"

—"*then thirty minutes ago Rosale Industries calls to explain they canceled their orders so they could reorder with a five-year ever-increasing contract! A friend of mine on Wall Street says the word is out about all our good luck and we're already selling at ninety-two!*"

The attorney paused before climbing into the taxi on Fifth Avenue. He peered up at Jamex's massive skyscraper. Perhaps it was just his imagination, but he thought one of the upper windows on the executive level was darker than it should be, almost as if a massive glob of protoplasm were pressed against the glass to glare out with a sinking kind of curious awareness. The attorney couldn't be sure he saw all that, but he laughed anyway as his cab drove off.

Example 2. "Yes siree bob!" exclaimed J. J. Wilkinson as he pulled the slightly soiled handkerchief across his forehead to remove sweat from the Florida sun. "You should have seen the place before we come to it. Hell of a deal it was back then. Just an old swamp, one of them kind you don't find much anymore, kind nobody ever used for something, full o' trees, smelly flowers, pools o' water, bears, maybe a few wolves, snakes 'n' gators, squawkin' birds, all kinds o' critters and strange things. Just a few old Seminoles living here. We got the lien on all the access property, and that, plus a little ol' friendly pressure and a few quick bucks, encouraged them Injuns to move on right quick. Didn't give us no real trouble and some good old boys up at the capital and in Washin'ton was glad to see us he'p 'em out.

"Didn't take Billy Joe and me more 'n three months to drain the swamp, fill in all them old holes, run off the critters, cut down the trees, pour the cement and whip the whole place into real fine shape. With all that money behind us from the Noo York banks, we got things moving real fine. One week we threw up all the houses, next week we put in the plumbing and the wiring, third week the detail stuff. By the end of the month all the recreational hoop-to-dos like tennis and shuffleboard courts every six blocks was almost finished. It's gotta be some kind of miracle, don't it? Last year this time there weren't nothing out here but a goddamn-pardon-my-French useless swamp, and now . . . Splendor City!! An all new condominium community with everything in tune and just right for fine folks like yourself!"

Steve and Judy Nelsen of Northfield, Minnesota, let their old but clear blue eyes follow J.J.'s sweeping motion as he pointed to the acres and acres of buildings called homes in the advertisements appearing in magazines read by the about-to-retire age group. Minnesota cold and an active life had kept Judy from wrinkling with the onslaught of the decades and when she gazed up at the towering figure of her husband, he could see her mouth form a frown of questioning uncertainty. J.J. could see it, too.

"Now, don't you go worrying none about your new homes. This here place is the nicest thing next to heaven! Safe, secure and quality-built. *Qual-i-ty!* Don't make no difference if you buy one of our Ramblin' Ranchets, the Spacious Split-level, the increasingly popular Towering Town House, the modest budget-priced Cozy Cottage, or the ever-popular Bright Bungalow, all our six thousand three hundred and twenty-two buildings are fully, unconditionally guaranteed for the rest of your lifetime or twenty years, whichever comes first. This ain't no fly-by-night retirement village, no siree bob. We stand by our work. And, as you know, any time during the first three years you want to sell back your house, we'll give exactly what you paid for it at no penalty. That's just one way we mean to attract and keep good-quality middle-class senior citizen folks like you from all over America who want a nice, quiet, safe, calm, serene place to spend those golden years. We just got started selling, but you know, I'm already so impressed by the caliber of folks we got here

100

that I know this community is going to go down in history for its special kind of people!"

Steve looked down at his wife. With his experienced eye J.J. read the "I'm-concerned-that-it-might-not-be-a-good-investment" look on his potential customer's face, and he quickly spoke to dispel any such fears.

"I know what you're thinking, and I don't blame you a bit," said the promoter as he shifted his stance and his tone into another well-practiced posture. "You're worried this whole thing might come apart, that it might not be a good investment. Now don't deny it, and don't be embarrassed or apologize for being cautious. I like a man who is cautious, even though I must admit most of our customers send us their initial checks right away after reading our brochures, and we ain't never had any complaints. Let me show you just how good of an investment this is.

"See those two men over there? The one who seems to be talkin' to himself all the time and the tall guy who looks like somebody you think you know? Damned if he don't look like this guy in an old movie me and Billy Joe watched on telebision last night while we wrote and told good folks like yourself that their dreams aren't too good to be true. Anyways, they're two big-shot investment brokers from some company named Sharing or some such dumb thing. They said me and Billy Joe should sell out our options and titles on Splendor City to them, and they were willing to pay us four and a half million, right here and now. Hell, that's almost three times what Billy Joe and I paid for the swamp, and a good million and a half over our construction costs.

"But you think Billy Joe and I took them up on their offer? Hell, no! We said, 'Mighty fine of you and thanks a lot, but we *believe* in Splendor City!' We have part of our lives tied up in this, and even if we didn't, we wouldn't sell out an investment like this for a few measly million. We told them they were welcome to buy some houses here, but not so many that good folks like you couldn't move in here. Kind of spoiled their morning right good it did, but me and Billy Joe, we got our integrity to think of.

101

"And, folks," said J.J. as he brought the soiled handkerchief out for another trip across his glistening brow, "that integrity is your guarantee in Splendor City, mark my word on it."

The Nelsens exchanged yet another long glance. The reluctance on Judy's face was beginning to wane when a cloud of dust appeared over the roofs of lot 49 and a metallic clatter drowned out the songs of the surviving bird. J.J. and the Nelsens squinted up the road at the growing ball of dust. J.J. momentarily forgot his confident sincerity and muttered, "Now what in the hell is *that*?"

Splendor City streets were paved only with promises. Contractual fine print explained the asphalt finish shown in the brochures was conditioned on an extra, unspecified fee. The ball of dust grew as it tore over dirt-packed Lindy Lane, cut east on Pleasant Avenue, then bore south on Sunshine Street directly to where J.J. and the Nelsens stood at the intersection of Sunshine Street and Bliss Avenue.

Three vehicles exploded from the dust cloud four blocks from J.J. and his customers. The first vehicle was a battered bullet-riddled 1959 Cadillac with one of the swooping rear fins shot off, the second was a 1969 pink and gray Rambler station wagon missing all its windows, while the third was a pickup truck of unidentifiable vintage tilting at an incredible angle of equilibrium. The machines roared, clattered and banged their way toward J.J. and his amazed customers. As they sped past the gawking trio, the pickup's rear fender almost hooked J.J.'s leg. J.J. heard the groan from the application of what were loosely termed brakes. Gravel crunched as the vehicles skidded to a stop one block away, all miraculously avoiding collisions with each other and the empty houses, although a utility pole disappeared under the pickup. The vehicles had barely completed the spinning turn before their motors roared again to race them toward J.J. and the Nelsens. This time the machines stopped three feet from the trio. The pickup caused no damage (there was none left to cause) when it crunched into the rear of the Rambler.

"Hey, man!" squealed a high-pitched voice from the dust

cloud after the sounds of slamming doors had ceased. "This here Splendor City?"

J.J. opened his dust-burned eyes to a nightmare. Standing in front of him was the caricature of the Times Square pimp, complete with black patent leather shoes, tight shiny black pants, plunging neckline purple shirt, a zoot suit, white blazer, snap-brimmed white hat, thick wraparound sunglasses and the blackest of the black skins J.J. had seen in all his cracker-coated fantasies. Behind the pimp stood the meanest humanoid Goliath from any of J.J.'s nighmares. J.J. couldn't help noticing the sawed-off shotgun the Goliath stuffed in his pants and the straight razor dangling from a thong round the monster's bulging neck, an instrument made incongrous by the Goliath's bristling, bushy blond beard.

"What . . ." began J.J. apprehensively. "Who are you?"

The pimp's high squeaky voice popped all of J.J.'s exotic plans of wealth. "I," said the pimp, "am John H27, and this here is my main man, John H96. We are the Tom Toms, and this here Splendor City is our new action center headquarters. Can you dig it, asshole?"

"Oh, my God," mumbled J.J. "Oh, my God."

"Not a bad place," continued John H27, "not bad at all. We weren't sure when we sent in our mail-order money, but what the hell. We bought us ten of your happy little bungalows scattered all through this here fun city, and we figure we gonna get to know our neighbors and they gonna get to know us. Gonna be an exciting place, long as nobody messes with us."

"Listen," J.J. said, doing his best to regain his sales composure, "I don't think you folks would be happy here. I mean really, why it's just not your kind of place at all. Not at all. I'll gladly refund all your money, plus some extra for expenses for your journey down here, and maybe. . . ."

"Shut up, mush face!" boomed John H96. His lips didn't seem to move when he spoke, nor did he shift his body, but J.J. could picture the blazing shotgun in his hands.

"Now we're going to take a look around," said John H27. "Then we'll be back to tell you what we think. We've scheduled a news conference for five o'clock with the networks so we can let everybody know we have arrived. You keep it cool or else my man H96 just might hate you a little more than normal."

The three vehicles roared away down Quiet Court. As the dust cloud receded, J.J. turned to look at the Nelsens. Their faces were shocked beyond expression. Before he could speak to them, a familiar voice hissed behind him and someone plucked at his elbow. J.J. whirled to see his partner, Billy Joe Mallard, crouched over from his usual lanky posture. The normally boisterous Billy Joe plucked meekly at J.J.'s elbow and timidly said, "J.J., come over here quickly, please! You have to see these gentlemen."

"Holy Christ, Billy Joe," began J.J., "you don't know what trouble we got. Our property values—"

"Don't bother with small problems now," hissed Billy Joe. "We don't have time. And for my mother's sake, be *very* nice to these men."

Billy Joe pushed his puzzled partner toward a trio of neatly dressed gentlemen. The leader of the trio stood in front of his two companions. The clean-cut leader reminded J.J. of the up-and-coming young vice-presidents from the New York banks who had helped him finance Splendor City. The other two visitors wore conservative clothes, but they made John H96 look like a sacrificial virgin. J.J. could bring himself to glance at their faces only once. His dominant impression was that of tank treads. Incongruously, the two neatly suited nightmares each carried a concert violin case. J.J. didn't think they looked like musicians.

"Mr. J.J. Wilkinson?" asked the trio leader pleasantly in what J.J. recognized as a salesman's tone. "My name is Smith. My two companions are Mr. Brown and Mr. Jones. We're local representatives of a very large family-owned national insurance firm and we are so pleased that you've decided to purchase one of our policies."

"Insurance? What are you talking about?" asked J.J. He looked at Billy Joe, but Billy Joe was looking toward heaven. "I didn't buy any insurance."

104

"Strictly speaking, that is correct," continued Mr. Smith. "You have yet to make your million-dollar payment."

"What the hell are you talking about?" demanded J.J. He quickly softened his tone when Mr. Brown coughed like a truck.

"Your first payment," continued Mr. Smith undaunted, "is due in one week. We will contact you with the details of the transaction. Of course, if you have no interest in the property you own, you needn't bother making the first payment. There would then be little need of a second payment as the value of whatever you have left to insure would be insignificant. As you are the owner, I'm sure you understand what I mean. Should you decide to be one of our happily insured family, please feel free to give me a call." Mr. Smith smiled at J.J. as he handed him a card on which was printed only a phone number.

"J.J.," said Billy Joe as the trio walked away, "we've got real trouble. We have to pay them or they'll destroy all our investment and we'll be broke. Or worse."

"They'll have a lot of competition to do that," replied J.J. grimly. He blinked, then whirled quickly, a homey "folks" already on his tongue. But the Nelsens had vanished, headed back to where Jesse James was a dead memory.

"What are we going to do, J.J.? What are we going to do?"

J.J. frowned while his partner raved. In the distance he saw two familiar figures turn the corner of Cheery Avenue and walk up Sunshine Street toward them. Hope flew back to J.J.'s commercial heart.

"Excuse me," he said as he approached the two men, his manner once again that of the salesman with the unbeatable product. "You two fellas still interested in picking up this once-in-a-lifetime development?"

The taller man seemed to shift somehow, and J.J. found himself talking to a firm, confident, easily recognizable sucker. "Maybe," said the archetype on cue. "Maybe."

"Well then," said J.J., "maybe we can do business. I only turned you down earlier so you would come back with a better offer. Since that time I've reconsidered, and I'm willing to let you take this sweet little number off our hands for your four and a half million right here and now."

The tall sucker looked at his balding, mumbling partner, then turned back to J.J. J.J. thought he saw a metamorphosis from sucker to unshakable, hard, successful bargainer before the taller man spoke. "Not a penny more than two million," said the confusing customer.

"You're crazy!" screamed J.J. involuntarily. "Why, we lose over half a million at that price."

"Take it or leave it," came the solid reply.

J.J. hesitated for a moment, then thought of the dust cloud and the insurance salesmen. "We'll take it," he said. "My backers have given me full authority to deal for them, but we have to make the transaction now, as soon as possible."

"I just happen to have some forms here which we can use," said the tall bargainer as he took some papers handed him by his mumbling companion.

Ten minutes later J.J. and Billy Joe were the ex-owners of Splendor City. They were hurrying up Sunshine Street to retrieve their belongings at the office when Mr. Smith caught up with them.

"Mr. J.J.! Mr. Billy Joe!"

They might have run for it, but they remembered the violin cases. Besides, Mr. Smith's voice seemed different, warmer.

"I'm glad I found you," panted Mr. Smith. He looked embarrassed and wouldn't meet their eyes. Almost as if he were afraid, thought J.J. "Upon reading your brochures more closely, I discovered the names of the New York banks that are involved with your fine operation here. It dawned on me that they are . . . well, that we and you are . . . well, what I'm really trying to say is that it seems you don't need our insurance after all. Please, please accept my apologies for any inconvenience my associates and I may have caused you. I'm very sorry, very sorry."

Apologizing profusely, Mr. Smith backed out of sight and out of their lives.

"How the hell do you figure that?" asked Billy Joe.

"I don't know," replied J.J., "and I don't think I want to know. But I'm still not sticking around here."

The dust cloud caught them at the corner of Sunshine Street and Blossom Avenue. John H27 stuck his snap-brim-hatted head out the Cadillac window to yell, "Hey, asshole! This place ain't got no opera house! How dumb can you get! We don't want to stay here. Hell, we ain't coming within a hundred miles of this place from now on. Here." John H27 threw a wad of paper from the car. "There's your deeds and bills of sale. You can keep that jive change we sent in as down payments. You'll need it when Reckoning Day comes 'round, baby. Bye!"

"J.J.," asked Billy Joe as the dust cloud roared away, "what the hell is happening to us?"

"I don't know, boy," replied his partner. "I don't know."

Their secretary met them at the door of the trailer house they used for an office. They could barely control her excitement enough to understand her story. "You mean you haven't heard!" she exclaimed. "Everybody in the town up the road is talking about it! Some geologists from Rosale Industries are poking around the county, and it looks like they've found major oil deposits! Even if there's no oil under Splendor City, our property values will skyrocket!"

J.J. hadn't run that far since the night Sheriff Birnbaum switched from rock salt to buckshot for garden raiders. He reached the tall man and his mumbling partner just as they were getting in their car.

"Hey, hey, hey," he wheezed at his last two customers. "You"—*pant pant*—"you boys aren't in a big hurry, are you?"

The two men looked at each other. Once again J.J. saw the tall man become the sucker. Being the salesman he was, J.J. just *knew* everything was going to be fine.

"Listen," said J.J., "I've been doing a little reconsidering. You know how us country boys are." He paused to catch his breath and wipe his slippery brow with his sopping handkerchief. "You boys wouldn't want to sell this tacky little housing development back to us, would you? I've kind of got an irrational hankering to peddle it myself."

The tall man frowned. He let J.J. sweat and shuffle in the dust for several minutes before he said, "Yup. Sell it back to you for four and a half million."

"You're crazy!" shouted J.J. "That gives you a two hundred and fifty percent profit for twenty minutes' worth of ownership. That's insane! That's downright dishonest!"

The tall man smiled slightly as if he were thinking of an old proverb. "You're right," he said, "that is a little too much. Make it an even four million. Not a penny less."

J.J. closed his eyes, wondered how he was going to explain all this in the boardrooms of the Noo York banks, then said, "It's a deal."

"I just happen to have adequate papers right here," said the tall man as he handed J.J. a pen and some papers passed him by his smiling, mumbling companion.

Fifteen minutes later J.J., Billy Joe and their not-for-long silent Noo York banking partners once again owned Splendor City. As J.J. watched the tall man's car with the Arizona license plate recede in the distance, he had the nagging feeling he had somehow, somewhere, missed something.

Example 3. Some say it was more than coincidence that the labor union held its annual convention in the Omaha meeting hall next to the hotel where famous entrepreneur-financier Geoffrey Regenstrief was vacationing fresh from his silicone-substitute coup, but then people say a lot of things. The important thing was that they were all there at the same time, entrepreneur Regenstrief, 4,322 labor leaders, with the usual sundry assortment of wives, friends, hookers and convention regulars, and the three hawkers working the parking lot between the convention center and the hotel, which was precisely where Geoffrey Regenstrief first saw them.

The blaring rock music first attracted him to their selling zone the way a fire attracts firemen, for Regenstrief hates blaring music, indeed, blaring noise of any nature. His two contradictory emotions are to flee from the painful tumult and to do his best to make it cease. Since his position and success have imbued him with almost unmitigated gall, he usually assumes he has only to protest for the latter course to be-

108

come a viable option. At any rate, Regenstrief charged into the parking lot to demand a cessation to the disturbing sound, then stayed to endure it for quite another reason, the reason which was the driving force of his life: money.

The blaring rock music came from a transistor radio carried by the young greasy-looking assistant to the main hawker. The noise repulsed Regenstrief, but he immediately grasped it's commercial application. The roar served as an attention-getting "white" noise drowning out the background and as a stunning device dulling customers' natural awareness, thus making them more susceptible to subliminal advertising. Major stores, especially large discount stores in shopping centers, use a similar technique with piped-in mindless music and bright glaring lights: Shoppers are bombarded audibly and visually until their equilibrium is shaken by their artificial environment. At that point the sales techniques of advertising, coupled with the crowd pressure to buy something, anything, make customers susceptible to exploitation. The audio technique works best when coupled with visual stimulation or stagnation (opposite ends of the same schtick). While an outdoor parking lot is hard to control visually, Regenstrief noted with professional approval that the head hawker was doing well with what he had. His second assistant was a stunningly beautiful, simply but carefully dressed black woman. Such visual beauty assaults everyone's senses with some emotion, and customer equilibrium is once again juggled. Sex, thought Regenstrief, is still one of the best sales techniques. He smiled again and turned his attention to the hawker and the sales pitch.

It took Regenstrief several seconds to convince himself that he really wasn't seeing a reincarnation of Albert Einstein standing behind the merchandise-laden table, a barker's cane substituted for the physicist's instructive piece of chalk.

"Hurry, hurry, hurry, while they last!" shouted the hawker. "Get your zonkers here! Only authorized outlet in the world for the incredible patented zonker! Mass sale of this incredible device will not begin for at least another six months. Get them now so you won't have to fight the rush.

The renowned zonker, beneficial to mental and physical health! Helps you give up that cursed smoking habit and have fun doing it without gaining weight! Provides a handy legal substitute smoking thrill for those of you into another type of inhalation. Great exercise for those of you who need it, yet little or no work involved! Helps facilitate your sex appeal and ability! Hurry, hurry, hurry, get them now while they last, only three dollars and sixty-nine cents!"

Regenstrief wanted to laugh at a business operating out of a suitcase with two assistants, selling what was probably an elaborate hoax most commercially hardened first graders would see through. But one thing kept Regenstrief from laughing: The crazy old hawker and his assistants were turning customers away. The two-bit street corner enterprise appeared on its way to becoming a million-dollar business. Regenstrief ran his practiced eye over the frantic, eager crowd. He had never seen people with such a compulsion to buy. Almost as if they were ordered or threatened, he thought.

A nearby church chimed fifteen minutes to five. Commuters were starting to return to their parking lot. The traffic began to interfere with the hawker's business. He reluctantly folded up his table, packed away his merchandise, and after repeatedly assuring frantic but frustrated customers that he would return the next day with a fresh supply of zonkers, he and his two assistants made their way to the hotel. Regenstrief followed them there. He approached their table in the coffee shop.

"Might I join you?" he asked.

The hawker glanced at his two associates, then shrugged. "Why not?"

After mutual introductions, during which Regenstrief noted that at least the hawker had heard of him, the financial wizard wasted no time.

"I couldn't help but noticing your success in the parking lot," remarked Regenstrief. "True, your methods are somewhat primitive and could be greatly improved upon and your product could bring in more money with national organization, but by and large I am impressed. And slightly curious. For example, just what is this zonker thing?"

The hawker smiled. His beautiful, lovely, talented, charming assistant handed him a small tube of wood about six inches long while his other assistant fiddled with the transistor radio to find another station. The hawker handed Regenstrief the zonker. The smooth wooden tube was thicker in the middle than on either end. A small hole was an inch from either end.

"What does it do?" asked Regenstrief, his curiosity overcoming his tendency never to admit ignorance.

"It does nothing," replied the hawker as he pushed his fluffy white frazzled hair back from his forehead. "You do *it*. Put one end, it doesn't matter which, in your mouth."

Regenstrief complied, feeling, for the first time in many years, rather silly.

"Now," commanded the hawker, "suck like it was a straw."

Regenstrief exhaled into the zonker as if it were a whistle.

"No, no!" remonstrated the hawker sharply and loudly enough for the other customers to turn their heads and stare at the group. "Don't blow! Suck! Suck!"

And much to his chagrin, Regenstrief sucked. A slight, almost inaudible whistle came from the two holes which were cut diagonally for a flutelike effect. Other than that, plus the rush of air into his lungs, Regenstrief noticed nothing.

"I don't understand," he said, a trace of anger creeping into his voice. "What does this do that you can sell it and make all those claims?"

The hawker smiled. "The health claim: You suck in a good deal of air. If you use the zonker regularly, it has an aerobic function. You can use it as a cigarette substitute to cut down on your smoking. If you use it enough and rapidly, you can hyperventilate, which, while not an altogether healthy thing, is basically harmless and produces a slightly giddy sensation which can be pleasurable. All that breathing, lung and mouth action burns up calories. How many we don't say, but obviously some weight could be lost. Some people claim they

111

can play music on the thing, thus imbuing the zonker with cultural worth. There's no end to its charms, uses and, I might add, profit."

Regenstrief stared at the hawker for several minutes. He began to laugh. "That's incredible! I don't believe it, but I've seen it work. You've got crowds of people out there buying this stupid thing, which can't cost over one dollar to make—"

"Eighty-four cents based on an hourly wage," interrupted the hawker.

"—and you'll be able to keep making money as long as you can find suckers . . . pardon the joke . . . to buy the dumb thing."

"It's the hula hoop of the future," commented the perceptive woman.

Regenstrief laughed and almost left. But when he remembered the crowds, he shifted his gaze back to the hawker. "Who controls this? Production, marketing, everything?"

"I do," replied the hawker. "Invented it myself from scratch. I hold patents, farm out the production, and I do my own merchandising."

Regenstrief frowned. It was stupid, but then again, if he only recouped half his expenses, the tax loss would help him on his total annual gross. It would take ten percent above expenses to turn a profit. There was a risk, true, but it was amusing, kinky, and . . . the crowds! He quietly said, "I'll buy the whole zonker thing from you for fifty thousand dollars now, ten thousand in two months."

"Wrong," said the hawker matter-of-factly.

"Wrong?" replied Regenstrief puzzledly.

"Wrong," stated the young male assistant as he turned down his radio.

"Most definitely wrong," said the wonderful woman firmly.

"What you will do," continued the hawker, "is buy the zonker empire from me for a flat one hundred thousand dollars. You won't own a thing until the check clears the bank and I see you haven't pulled a fast one on us."

112

The hawker's announcement stunned Regenstrief. As he sat there looking at the madman, he heard rock music blare and felt the light bounce off all the highly polished chrome in the café—sugar container tops, napkin dispensers, salt-and-pepper shakers, table edging, coat trees, all augmented by the bright sunlight streaming through the windows. Being a fairly normal male, he felt the exotic presence of the girl. Amid the incongruity of his situation danced visions of mass-marketing schemes, promotional contests, mail-order franchising, retail merchandising and wholesale outlet subsidiaries. It was too much for one man to take.

"Done," he said, reaching for his checkbook.

"Make it out to Charon Enterprises, Inc.," said the hawker.

And so it was that the next morning Regenstrief and a hastily assembled crew of professional salesmen, beautiful models, equipment-ladened technicians, and a public relations/press corps descended on the parking lot. The labor convention had adjourned the night before, but Regenstrief (who has a streak of romance in him) reasoned that with the reputation the zonker must have already established, plus its innate worth, he would have a busy fun morning selling the item the original way before he went into the nationwide campaign.

At the end of two hours of hard-core selling with modern techniques, Regenstrief, masterful entrepreneur that he was, had sold six zonkers, two of them on credit. A police cruiser had pulled into the lot, followed by an official-looking sedan with "Environmental Control Office—Noise Pollution Bureau" emblazoned on the front doors. Regenstrief heard the roar of a departing jet; then he looked at the horde of beautiful but bored models, apprehensive salesmen, puzzled technicians and embarrassed PR assistants. For some reason, the famous financial wizard Geoffrey Regenstrief just had to laugh.

Those are but three stories I could tell to illustrate this phase of The Plan. Our consortium with the "Big Three" op-

113

erated through a front called Charon Investments. In addition to these three examples and numerous other "special" projects he directed, Donnely used Charon Investments to play what he called "the standard economic market." With the tips and knowledge supplied by Rosale, Kearns, Valentine and their associates, Donnely masterminded dozens of orthodox financial coups.

Things looked up for Donnely and me personally, too. After the first week and a couple of successes, we were transferred to the maximum security block where our partners stayed. The warden saw to it we had private cells complete with double beds, private showers, cooking facilities and a stereo FM radio-record player and black-and-white TV home entertainment center. We didn't rate quite as high as Kearns, Rosale or Valentine, but the warden trusted us more than John H1. All we had to do was give the screws an occasional market tip. We wouldn't have had to do that, for now we had clout.

My life in particular began to get better. I spent mornings working with Donnely on the projects. We spent most of our afternoons reading in the library. He insisted on helping me choose books, starting me with Copi's *Introduction to Logic* and a Rex Stout murder mystery. He said the first one would help me develop my already fine mind and the second one would keep me amused. He was right, but then he always is.

Syndicate boss Kearns must have taken a liking to me. He insisted that I call him Wally. And he came to see me one Thursday night a month into the operation.

For a while I thought I had been afflicted by the occupational disease of criminals who get caught: I thought I was stir crazy. Why? I found reason number two sitting on my couch after dinner, her long blond hair cascading over her shoulders and brushing the soft, almost sheer material of the white negligee which was all she was wearing at the time. I was afraid, both in case she was a hallucination and in case she wasn't.

"Hi, Jack," she said sweetly and pleasantly as she rose to

114

meet me, her firm ripe form moving slightly under the loose bits of material. "My name is Ginger. I'm Wally's niece. He said you were lonely and I thought it would be only human of me to come see if I couldn't cheer you up."

I hate to interrupt this scene at this particular poignant point, partially because it's such a nice memory and partially because I am sure I have aroused your intellectual interest. However, an explanation is needed, and although I'm not sure this is the most aesthetically pleasing place to render it, I can't find another more suitable location.

Everyone in the prison knew about Wally's phenomenally large family and the way he got to see them in his private suite, er, cell. This knowledge didn't do much for prisoner morale. Wally's brothers and sisters must have been unusually prolific, for Wally has a huge number of nieces. They were always coming to visit their uncle. Occasionally, like at least twice a week after the first visit, Wally would send one of his nieces down to meet me. I don't know if Donnely ever met any of Wally's nieces because we never talked about it. I have my suspicions, though. The nieces I met varied a lot. Wally had redheaded, blond and brunet nieces of all shapes and sizes. One of his nieces who visited me was a cute, giggly Chinese girl and another could have been Meredith's (I thought about her a lot) cousin. Wally's nieces all had two things in common. The first one was their desire to make sure I wasn't . . . lonely. The other thing they had in common they shared with their uncle Wally, which of course is often the case with relatives: It was kind of funny, but none of them looked Jewish.

Now where was I? Oh, yes. . . .

When niece Ginger quit walking, she was only inches from my trembling body. I looked down into her laughing blue eyes. She wasn't wearing any perfume and I could smell her natural womanliness. I could feel her body heat. She was the first member of the opposite sex I had seen in over two months. I hadn't "been involved" with anyone for more than a year.

What would you do? I came apart at the seams. I surrendered myself to her ministering comforting. But I must admit, what with feeling as I did about Meredith, my heart wasn't completely in it.

I often wondered why Mr. Kearns—I mean, Wally—threw those pebbles in my pond.

The Pull-Off

On the morning of the ninety-seventh day of the consortium's short life and the hundred and forty-fifth day of our incarceration in Havensbrook federal maximum security prison, a Friday, Donnely and I were suntanning on the roof of the death house. They have yet to use the death house for its official purpose. The prison builders threw in an electric chair in case executions make a comeback, so a combination of anticipation and tradition gave our sunning building its name. I had just rolled over on my back to do my front, the part of suntanning I hate most because you can't read or do anything but lay there with the hot sun beating down on you and hurting your eyes despite the wraparound sunglasses and closed eyelids, when one of the cons working for the consortium brought up a batch of ticker tape for Donnely. The con also brought my copy of the New York *Times*.

I didn't look at the *Times* just then because as I said, I was sunning my front. I vaguely remember Donnely handing the con a note. Donnely later told me it was a teletype message for Charon Investments' broker. The warden immediately transmitted it over the nationwide criminal identification teletype network and the New York cop on the other end, one of Wally's longtime employees, picked up the phone and called the broker. Ten minutes later the broker called him back, the cop transmitted the message to the warden, and the warden sent a screw up to give it to Donnely. Electronic communications are a marvel.

Donnely briefly read the note; then he went back to his book. Those of you who are trivia historians may want to note that the book was Charles G. Finney's classic, *The Circus of Dr. Lao.* Donnely had to get the warden to special order it from the Library of Congress. Donnely read the two remaining pages, closed the book and stretched out on his back.

"How you doing, Jack?" Donnely casually inquired.

"Oh, OK," was my easy reply.

"Do you want me to buzz for some lemonade or anything?"

I thought for a moment, then said, "No, I'll be OK until we go for lunch. How about you?"

"Oh," he said easily, "I think I'll be OK. I just was wondering."

"Thanks," I said. Donnely really is basically a considerate guy.

"Oh, that's OK. Say, Jack?"

"Hmmm?"

"How are you coming?"

"What do you mean, Dan?"

"With your reading and things."

"Pretty good, I guess. I'll probably finish *Gravity's Rainbow* by the end of next week. It's taking me awhile."

"Yeah, I know what you mean. Took me awhile, too. You getting enough rest?"

That was an indirect reference and hint. The reference was to Wally's nieces' visits. The reference implied they might be tiring me slightly and keeping me from devoting enough energy to my reading. It seems those visits were fairly well known. I got a rather cryptic postcard from Larry as my cousin Paul who was visiting Chicago. The postcard merely read, "Wish I was there, relatively speaking, of course." I didn't like that at all, but there was nothing I could do. Cons are helpless people. Daniel's hint was that I should be careful how I ordered my priorities. I had learned a lot by then about analytical reasoning, or so I thought. "Oh," I said, underplaying his move, "I'm getting enough."

"That's good," he replied.

We lay there for a few minutes in silence. I could faintly hear marching feet in the exercise yard and a meadowlark was singing from on top of Cellblock C. I almost fell asleep.

118

"Jack?"

"Ummm?" I was almost irritated that Donnely had broken into my dreams.

"Do you have anything pressing you want to do here in the next couple of weeks?"

I didn't understand that, but then I was only half listening. "No," I replied, trying to hold on to the sleeplike euphoria our conversation was driving away.

"Then you think you could finish up whatever you have going here by the end of next week?"

That registered. I slowly raised up until I was propped on my elbow, looking at Daniel's lanky brown form stretched out on the air mattress to my left. I took off my sunglasses and said, "Daniel James Donnely, what are you driving at?"

"Well," he said matter-of-factly, "I just wondered if you would be ready to leave prison by the end of next week."

"What!" I jerked so fast my sunglasses fell from my hand, cracking one of the hand-ground lenses. They were specially made and a present from Harold Rosale.

"Yeah," said Donnely calmly. He didn't even shift position. "I just finished the last book I couldn't get on the Outside and with the sale our broker just put through, Charon Investments, Inc., has made a $16,831,432 net profit since its inception. We're well over the hump and I figure we might as well close up the operation and go home. If that's OK with you."

Nervous disbelief kept my voice under control. "You mean you've fixed it so we can get out of prison now? I mean next week? Not in twenty-nine years?"

Daniel shifted slightly, but he still stared straight up at the sky. "Well, everything but the minor details. That's why I said next week. It might take that long. Shall we shoot for Thursday so we can be with The Group on the weekend?"

Everyone in the prison heard my scream.

The next morning Donnely and I had a conference with an assistant Arizona attorney general, a gubernatorial aide, President Morris Sylvester of the First State Citizens' Bank of Hamilton, Arizona, an FBI agent and our able attorney, the

119

Professor. We used the warden's reception room. I was a little woozy, having spent the night with one of Wally's Oriental nieces celebrating a very special Chinese New Year. My Lee has the energy of an entire Chinese Red Army battalion. I kept fading in and out of the conversation, so my record may not be completely accurate.

"Let me repeat your offer, just to make sure I've got it clear, all right, Mr. Donnely?" The governor's aide was speaking. "You and Mr. Mason are saying the rest of your gang will turn themselves in, along with the equivalent amount of money stolen from the bank, plus a flat five percent interest contribution, in exchange for, and here I'm quoting from your counsel's brief, 'a full and complete pardon for any and all crimes committed by those persons'—meaning you and your gang—'prior to the date of the bank's reimbursement.' Is that correct?"

Donnely, just to be sure, looked to the Professor. After our counselor nodded, Donnely told the aide he was correct.

"And the alternative, as I understand it," continued the aide, "is that no money will be returned, no further members of your gang will surrender, your attorney will institute some rather elaborate appeal proceedings, and you will institute a type of public relations information campaign. Right?"

Donnely answered very carefully. "Well, sir, I think you have given a fairly accurate interpretation of the only legal choices we see open to us if our offer is refused."

The governor's aide looked at us critically over his horn-rimmed glasses. "Isn't that a piece of black—"

"Tell me, counselor," interrupted the Professor quickly, addressing the attorney general's man, "did you ever study the laws regarding slander and defamation of character?"

The governor's aide looked at the Professor and smiled. The Professor smiled back.

"We'll let that go," said the aide. "Tell me, Mr. Sylvester, it was your bank which was robbed. How do you feel about this?"

Sylvester had lost quite a lot of weight since I had last seen him. His jowls were now merely flaps of skin. He still

120

mopped his brow with his handkerchief, though, and he did so now. "Well, well," he anxiously said. "Well. Well, sir, as you may know, our bank ownership has recently changed hands. I was informed yesterday that our new owners, Apollo Industries, Inc., have no wish to see anyone in jail for that rather unfortunate incident some months ago. I informed them this morning of Mr. Donnely's offer and they told me it suited their plans admirably. Admirably."

The governor's aide shrugged his shoulders. "Well, then, what can I say? The governor yesterday afternoon also received several favorable recommendations concerning this matter. Since the bank has no objections and the money is being returned and since we will be able to identify all the guilty parties before they become innocent again, I am empowered to say the state is satisfied with the matter. Of course, it will take a few days for the paperwork, but shall we say . . . next Thursday?"

And so it was that on that Thursday The Group, including the Professor but excluding Donnely and me, marched into the First State Citizens' Bank of Hamilton, Arizona, and surrendered both themselves and $787,532.68 in cash to local authorities. They were immediately arrested for bank robbery. Under armed guard they walked to the courthouse, pleaded guilty, were arraigned before the same judge who sentenced Donnely and me, convicted, sentenced to thirty years and then freed by judicial order acting on receipt of a full and complete pardon for each of them. The whole process took just under an hour.

While they were in court, John H1 and his drum brother John H9 were fitting me with a graduation suit, the same thing the state of Arizona gives all its released cons. I waived the twenty-five dollars and a bus ticket to the Arizona city of my choice, telling the warden to contribute the money to a private foundation which runs halfway houses for ex-cons. After I bid a fond farewell to the drum brothers in the prison tailor shop—"Later, you pieces of pig dung"—I joined Donnely in the warden's reception room. He wasn't alone.

"On behalf of my colleagues," said Wally jovially as we

121

sipped the warden's cognac, "I would like to say that it has not only been a financially rewarding experience to work with you two gentlemen, it has been a fascinating, instructive, entertaining pleasure. All my colleagues want me to assure you that the consortium as a group and we as individuals will respect all terms of our agreement, and, as they say in the Yard, you are 'cool [*i.e.,* safe].'

"Now that my official mission is finished, I shall become quite personal. You two gentlemen are unique. I have enjoyed your company and I shall look forward to watching your progress. If at any time you feel you might like to assist me in my work, rest assured my associates and I will welcome you into the fold like long-lost nephews."

He must have realized neither Donnely nor I had aspirations to work for organized crime, for he smiled as he said that. With a final nod he turned and left the office. When he opened the door, I got what I thought was my last glimpse of Bruno.

Donnely smiled at me and I smiled back. We drank a last silent toast with the warden's cognac and pushed the button for our escort. The warden himself entered. With the cheers of cons and screws ringing in our ears and accompanied by the head screw, we walked through all those locked doors. When the last one closed behind us, we were alone. Then we crossed the parking lot to where the rest of The Group and freedom waited.

The Pushover

The ride back to Hamilton, Arizona, was frantic. Everyone yelled and talked at once, laughing, giggling and drinking champagne. Everyone except Meredith. And me, whenever I turned around and saw her lovely form sitting sulking in the corner of the ancient Rolls hearse Larry, Raoul and Alfred converted into a limousine for The Group.

She had acted strangely from the start. I had been trying to resign myself to the fate of her and Donnely ever since I heard we were getting out. The euphoria of our pending release, plus the ministerings of Wally's nieces, had helped a little, but once we were free, I was back on my own. The others kept me gay, at least on the outside. As I laughed, I proceeded to get as drunk as I could.

Meredith had been acting strangely ever since we first saw The Group. She had been in the front line of the running melee which greeted us. I expected her to run into Donnely's eager arms, so I dropped back and let him precede me. She greeted him first, somewhat coldly I thought, all things considered. Maybe she was miffed at him for something. Then she looked around him and stared at me. After a few seconds she coldly said, "Hello, Jack." She looked at me as if I were garbage, then walked away. When we reached the old mansion The Group was renting, she ran into the house before the rest of us reached the porch.

Donnely found me in the corner about half an hour later. I wasn't anywhere near drunk yet, but I was working hard at it and getting closer every second. The victory party swirled around us, dancing to the sounds of Raoul's transistor radio and punctuated by Larry's mumblings.

123

"Why are you here by yourself, Jack?" Donnely asked.

Sometimes when I drink and feel blue, I get belligerent. I snapped back at him. "Why are you by yourself? Where's the lovely Meredith? Why aren't you with her, old buddy?"

Donnely frowned and looked at me for a long time. Then he pulled up a chair and practically sat on top of me.

"Jack, remember when you asked me once what your specialty was? Remember that? Do you still want to know?"

I looked at him, extremely interested but too angry, hurt and stubborn to admit it. "Why not? It will be better than chatting about what we'll do with our security and jobs with Apollo Industries."

Donnely smiled and shook his head. I felt horrible.

"Jack," he said, "think back to the day Frank Douglas was killed. Remember? That stupid intelligence officer didn't believe us dumb ground-pounding Marine enlisted men knew what we were talking about, so he sent you and Frank out with a patrol to check out what the three of us already knew. When the VC hit the patrol and killed the sergeant and Frank, you were the one who kept your head, who somehow pushed everybody else back to safety. That's your specialty, Jack. You're solid as a rock, the most solid, dependable, thoughtful person I know. You're solid, but not unbendable. The kind of guy who could serve as a stable nucleus for a bunch of unstable geniuses. You also have other things going for you, like ignorance of your talents, which keeps you from getting haughty and losing them, a fairly developed sense of humanity—remember the goon you should have knifed but didn't?—and a fair sense of humor. But your one drawback is that so much of the time you don't give yourself any credit and you keep your stone-solid head in the clouds.

"Now don't you think I know you're crazy about Meredith? Don't you think everybody—except Meredith—knows you're crazy about her? Meredith thinks you don't have any time for her and that hurts her, because she's crazy about you, too."

"Bullshit," I said, a little of the belligerence still in me.

Donnely just sadly shook his head. I could have taken it better if he hit me. "Jack," he said, "think about it. Larry tried to tell you before we hit the bank, but you were too dense to take the hint. Hell, Meredith as much as told you herself in Larry's first letter to the prison, remember?"

"Yeah," I said, defending a position I didn't want to be true, "she told you to take very good care of yourself. I was only supposed to be careful."

One of the most vexing things about Daniel James Donnely is that he has total recall. "Listen a minute," he said. "This is what she said, through Larry's words: 'Well, she (Meredith) says for you (Jack) to take good care of yourself and to tell your friend (me) to be very sure to do the same.' See?"

"Yeah," I said, "see!"

"Idiot!" Donnely was getting impatient. "I was supposed to do the same thing you were. 'Take very good care' of *you*." He stood up and looked down at me with what I thought was contempt but what he later told me was only anger. "Well, I've done about all I can do."

With that he stormed away to talk to Alfred.

Have you ever felt as if someone had pulled the plug on your stagnant pond and you were slowly oozing away? Have you ever felt that if someone called you worthless, you would feel complimented? Have you ever felt like scum? If you have, you have a good idea how I felt for about five minutes as I sat in that corner considering things. But right in the middle of my wallow I saw a light. There might be, just might be, hope.

I put my champagne glass down without draining it. I didn't want any more alcohol, which might muddle my already sticky situation. I slowly stood and went looking for Meredith.

I found her in about the twentieth room I looked in, a bedroom way at the back of the house. She was sitting on the bed, looking out the window at nothing in particular. When I came in, she whirled around. Her bloodshot eyes fastened briefly on me and then looked at something I couldn't see on the floor.

"Ah, Meredith . . ." I began in my own inimitable, suave, unconquerable style.

"Is there something I can do for you, Jack? I figured you would be busy at the party or maybe with some kind of 'family' reunion, or have all those 'nieces' left you too tired?"

When Meredith is hurt or mad, she can be as tough and cutting as a good razor blade. She also bends and breaks easily, however.

I knew that if I tried long, detailed explanations right away, I would trip over my tongue and blow the whole thing. So I plowed straight ahead. I walked over to her and pulled her (almost roughly, she says) up off the bed. I held her incredibly soft, trembling and very surprised body six inches away from my trembling form while I talked. Actually touching her and having her that close after all those months of dreaming almost made me lose my nerve right then and there, but inertia kept me rolling ahead.

"Meredith," I said with a great deal of effort, "some time later we'll talk about a lot of things. One of those things is relativity, how important some things are in relation to others. Right now all I have to say is you are and you have been and always will be the most important thing in my life."

A startled look crossed her already surprised face. She didn't say a word, she just stood there looking at me for a few seconds. Then as a funny type of half-smile formed on her tremendous mouth and a single tear trickled down her smooth black cheek, I folded her into my arms.

About fifteen minutes later I was vaguely aware of Donnely shutting the door. I think some others were with him, but I wasn't paying any attention and neither was Meredith.

PHASE III

The Preliminaries

Shortly after Donnely and I got out of prison, we joined the other members of The Group as employees of the business we owned, Apollo Industries, Inc. In true American tradition we started at the top. Donnely was president and chairman of the board of directors and I was vice-president and secretary to the board of directors. The Professor was chief counsel to both the company and the board of directors. The rest of The Group made up the board of directors and held jobs in the company. Alfred was head of the Research Division and gleefully presided over one of the largest labs in the Southwest. Larry was in charge of the Technical Development Division. He was also chairman of the Hamilton, Arizona, Red Cross Canteen Association. Meredith, my lovely Meredith, partner in what prudish-but-accepting Alfred calls "living in sin" (we decided to go slowly with our "relationship"), was in charge of Advertising and Promotions. Reginald ran the Personnel Department in what *Time* magazine called "an unorthodox fashion," letting our employees decide such things as wages, hours and benefits for themselves while he spent most of his time practicing his characters, which suited us fine, since we don't manage people as a matter of routine. Raoul wanted to be in charge of the secretary pool and employee relations, but Reginald, the Professor and Donnely wisely vetoed that. For one thing, they wanted him to continue his law studies with the Professor. For another thing, there was his problem which he hadn't burned out with the starlets. Arizona is full of bored granddaughters of wealthy retirees and they were sapping enough of his strength. Raoul served as assistant to the general counsel.

You might have the same basic question the special Senate investigating committee had—namely, what did (does) Apollo Industries do? The answer is simple. It makes money.

Donnely had always been careful to give Alfred as much time as possible to work on his ideas. Donnely set the criteria for what Apollo needed to be a successful company; then he assigned Alfred to come up with the entity and Larry to help Alfred refine it. They succeeded one week before we got out of prison. With the money from our investments, a little knowledgeable pressure learned in prison and the Marines and his natural genius, Donnely created what economists call a self-generating vertical monopoly.

The orders Donnely gave Alfred were to find a simple, easy-to-make, cheap invention which could be built as an indispensable unit of the existing economy and constructed from materials which could be controlled by Apollo Industries.

Of course, if something indispensable to the American economy was not then in existence, then the American economy could not have been functioning. That's a simple matter of deductive definition. Donnely knew that. So what he had to do was redefine indispensability to include Apollo's product. That was Meredith's area of expertise. Donnely and I helped her as much as we could.

Alfred worked very hard to come up with just the right thing. He ran literally thousands of experiments, developed (with some degree of success) hundreds of new items and went through a large portion of the company's assets before he and Larry finally found the Whirlathon.

Surprised, aren't you? I bet you didn't know that The Group was responsible for the Whirlathon wonder which now keeps your car running safely and economically like the marvelous machine that it is. Well, that just goes to show you how much Donnely and The Plan contribute to America. If this were England, we probably would be knighted and lunch with the queen.

For those of you who aren't mechanically minded, let me explain just what a Whirlathon is. As Meredith's advertising copy "discovered," mud and man-made pollution create a problem when they stick to a car's tire housing. It doesn't make any difference what model car, the problem is still there. Of course, no one *really* knows how much of a problem this constitutes, but then since a problem is not defined on the basis of universal criterion but rather on perceived opinion, if enough of the right people say there's a problem, then there's a problem. How many gallons of gasoline were needlessly consumed by car engines laboring to pull the extra weight of tire casing coatings? How many lives were lost in accidents where casing coating played a role? How many millions of dollars' damage does unchecked casing coating cause each year? Why wasn't something done about the casing coating before?

The answers to all but the last question are open to debate. The answer to the last question is simple: Before The Plan and Apollo, no one had the Whirlathon.

Meredith used a variety of articles, ads and announcements in trade and technical journals to discover the coating problem. She even let the New York *Times* and the Washington *Post* "uncover" the unprotected car casing scandal. Then, before the iron got hot enough to induce another entrepreneur to strike, Apollo announced it had invented and was producing the Whirlathon to solve the coating problem. Basically, the Whirlathon is a scientifically designed and engineered (heavy words in American commerce) strip of metal attached to the axle which turns with the tire, scraping the coating off the inside of the casing before it has a chance to build, thereby solving the problem of coating on the casing, eliminating the symptomatic drag and facilitating (carefully chosen word, that) improved gas mileage, safety and vehicle operating life. Isn't modern technology marvelous? Under the ironclad patent on the Whirlathon drawn up jointly by the Professor, Alfred, Larry, Donnely and myself, the only place you can buy a device to relieve your casing coating problem is at or through Apollo Industries.

Apollo Industries makes Whirlathons out of minerals quarried at a site in Arizona (owned by Hermes, Inc., a wholly owned subsidiary of Apollo), discarded car bodies (collected and processed by ReCycle, Inc., a subsidiary of Acme Salvage,which is controlled by Apollo) and aluminum imported from South American companies on Trans-Quick ships. Trans-Quick Industries and Shipping, Inc., is owned by Comet Enterprises, a partially owned, completely controlled subsidiary of the First State Citizens' Bank of Hamilton, Arizona. Apollo bought the bank long before the Whirlathon. The bank also holds stock in several foreign mining firms. In the rare event (Donnely knows who to bribe) the foreign sources become belligerent in their business dealings with Apollo, the company can sever its "dependency" of them, develop the more-than-adequate domestic supplies and profitably write the whole thing off in taxes as a business loss. As it is, Apollo and friends reap a fine profit, using the foreign investments and foreign tax credits as write-offs for American tax purposes. The end product of Whirlathons are sold through a retail outlet called Service, Inc., owned jointly by Hamilton's leading bank and the Selectric Investment Firm (which is owned by Apollo Industries), to service stations and automotive centers and through a wholesale enterprise formed by an attorneys' consortium directed out of a small legal firm in Beaver Crossing, Nebraska.

Immediately after developing the Whirlathon, Apollo Industries "went public" and sold forty-five percent of its shares, in various lump blocks, to the major car manufacturers, New York banks and national investment firms, thus ensuring a sound financial interest base. Before the Whirlathon was marketed by Apollo Industries, the First State Citizens' Bank of Hamilton invested its funds heavily in common stocks of the major auto companies and sent a representative to the stockholders' conventions of those companies. Using a combination of sales techniques, stock manipulation and political pressure, Apollo persuaded the major auto companies to make Whirlathons standard features on all models.

As you can probably tell, Apollo Industries makes substantial profits on several levels. Besides the interlocking service

132

system I have described, Donnely worked out a number of related, profit-turning services. But everything revolved around the Whirlathon. Eventually, the whole system became self-sustaining and the profits really poured in. Beautiful, huh?

Now I don't mean to leave the impression that the "Apollo miracle" as it was described last month in *U.S. News & World Report* occurred overnight. It took well over six months for Donnely and The Group to build Apollo into the multimillion-dollar corporate conglomerate that it is.

At the end of those six months things looked pretty good for The Group: As legitimate citizens we all had incomes far exceeding our expectations and rapidly approaching our wildest dreams. Donnely and the Professor directed our financial investments in such a way that, barring a world economic catastrophe of unparalleled dimensions, we will be comfortably secure as long as we live. In that event Apollo has built and provisioned several secret "survival centers" scattered strategically across the globe. Alfred, Larry and Donnely designed the centers so The Group, if we get to the centers (Donnely figures we have a seventy-five to twenty-five chance of reaching them in time), has a fifty–fifty chance of weathering any catastrophe.

By the seventh month of operation most of us had little to do besides shuffle paper and keep our eyes open. Of course, Alfred and Larry were involved in innumerable projects, so they didn't notice the slack in activities, and the Professor and budding lawyer Raoul were busy with academe. But Meredith and I (even though our bliss was still reaching new heights), Donnely and Reginald were beginning to spend a lot of time talking to each other and avoiding awestruck executives who kept "popping down" to visit our Arizona facility, hoping to learn how to do it for their companies, too.

One of the ways we had of dodging them was to spend time in our branch office in Chicago. Only The Group knew Apollo had a Chicago branch, which is one reason we started one. Everyone in The Group liked to get away now and then for privacy.

Apollo's real Chicago headquarters stands one block west

133

of Clark Street in Chicago's Near North Side, a hodgepodge middle-income area just turning into a swinging-stewardess-young-single-executive-glitter neighborhood. Clark Street is the business row with shops, cafes and small firms scattered along the two sides. Our headquarters is on a corner, a huge, rambling four-story building completely surrounded by a ten-foot brick wall topped with barbed wire and broken glass. The electrically charged heavy iron gates can withstand the push of a ten-ton truck or a shell from a Sherman tank. The grounds are small, but the mansion does have a lawn of its own. Specially designed mines, pressure alarms and similar security devices wait beneath the grass. Besides the main gate and front pedestrian passage through the wall, a secret tunnel connects the mansion with a dimly lit bar one block away. The bar caters to prostitutes, pimps and perverts, most of whom have an out-of-character undying loyalty to Donnely. Don't ask me how he met them, let alone how he turned them into staunch allies. That's just Donnely.

The real Chicago headquarters was built by a paranoid financier who died of starvation avoiding poison he thought his relatives were putting in his food. It was lucky for him that he didn't eat his food, because they actually were poisoning it. After their uncle died, the heirs sold the house to a religious group because the family didn't have any use for an urban fortress equipped with the latest in security devices. The religious group, the Crucibles, didn't have any use for the security devices either, but they did need a house with forty-three rooms to house their communal congregation. The Crucibles believed that a union of the Mohican sun-god, Moses and the soul of their dead founder ruled the earth through a series of predetermined cycles. Crucibles supported themselves by begging and baking poppy seed cakes. Last January the head Crucible had a vision that the world was going to end on February 3 and in a sense he was right. In the early-morning hours of that day he and the entire congregation of Crucibles rented wooden boats and rowed out to a point in Lake Michigan just north of Gary, Indiana, to watch the sun come up one last time. The sun rose at 7:15. At

8:01 Omega Steel, Inc. (in no way connected to Apollo Industries), tested a new water purification device for their drainage system into the lake. The device failed and the effluent washed untreated into Lake Michigan, where an undertow carried it to the calm section of water on which the boats of the Crucibles rested peacefully. Before dissipating, the effluent dissolved the wooden rowboats and all other organic material it touched. So ended the world for the Crucibles.

Meredith and I have had several long discussions trying to determine who threw the Crucibles' pebbles into Lake Michigan's effluent-filled pond. We haven't agreed on anyone yet.

Donnely had the Professor quietly untangle the estate of the Crucibles and buy the house in the name of G. Orevidal as a private residence. No one besides The Group knew about the G. Orevidal residence. Anyone who pursues his curiosity about the mansion discovers G. Orevidal is a wealthy recluse painter whose works are largely held by private collectors and a few museums. Donnely "created" G. Orevidal long before Apollo. I know Donnely used that identity in some sort of art scam, but he's always vague on details. Donnely had Larry and Alfred make sure the facilities in the house, including the elaborate security devices, were in tiptop working order, and he furnished a suite of apartments for each of us. Donnely turned one of the rooms into a darkroom for Meredith, made a workroom for Larry, a dressing room for Reginald, a study room-visitors' boudoir for Raoul, a greenhouse for the Professor, a small lab for Alfred and a library for the two of us. Reginald sometimes uses the small briefing room-auditorium-movie theater to practice his characters. Chicago became our quiet escape from the hustle and bustle of Hamilton, Arizona.

Some of Donnely's arrangements in connection with the house, especially his making sure the security arrangements were in excellent shape, should have tipped me off, but they didn't. He later admitted the probabilities of Phase III had been an influential factor in The Group's acquisition of the G. Orevidal residence.

I was actually the first one to stumble across Phase III. Or rather, to have Phase III walk in on me. Meredith was there, too, but it was me that Phase III came to, which caused me some trouble with Meredith.

I was sitting behind my massive mahogany desk in the Arizona headquarters of Apollo Industries, Inc., trying to make three in a row in the basketball contest I played against the wastepaper basket, my own bad aim and prevailing winds from the central temperature treatment unit. I had just wadded the piece of paper into the right size when my phone rang. I let it ring five times before I answered it and, when I finally picked up the receiver, my voice was irate: The ringing had broken my concentration and cost me the shot.

"Excuse me for disturbing you, sir," said Edward, my snooty secretary and former Harvard Graduate School of Business valedictorian, "but there is a young lady wishing to see you. Shall I send her in?"

Rather than ask Edward for any details, I said yes. That was stupid. I certainly didn't expect the person who walked through the main door to be *that* young lady. I should have asked Edward who it was, so I could have prepared myself. Of course, she had a plausible lie ready to tell Edward, but I should have asked anyway.

Meredith, as radiant as ever, came in through the door connecting our offices just before the main door opened. I still had that special smile on my face when in walks My Lee.

Remember My Lee? Wally's niece with the energy of a Chinese Red Army battalion? Needless to say, Meredith was somewhat cool to the cute little Oriental girl when I made the introductions and explanations.

My Lee wasn't as effervescent as she was in our earlier encounters, which was probably lucky for everyone concerned, since Meredith might have tried to pop her bubble. Meredith is very jealous sometimes. In fact, My Lee was downright morose.

"Oh, Mr. Jack," she said in her halting English. Wally likes his nieces to be really Oriental if they are Oriental. "Bad news, very bad news."

136

She didn't have to tell me. By this time I knew something was wrong. For one thing, I had never expected to hear from anyone connected with the old Charon consortium again. For another, I knew My Lee wouldn't have come to me for help with any personal problems. I tried to keep calm as I said, "What do you mean?"

"Oh, Uncle Wally, he very sick. He say, go tell Jack and Donnely man there big trouble brewing and they come see him right away quick. Right away quick, he say. Uncle Wally say for you to come with me and bring Donnely with you. He say that make it OK with your woman then, for chaperon thing all fixed up. You come, please?"

What could I do? Donnely, My Lee and I caught the next plane.

I should explain what happened to the rest of the consortium. Most of the information I have came from Wally at that meeting. They all got out of Heaven within two months after Donnely and I were pardoned, but let's take them individually.

Harold Rosale was the last of the consortium to leave the pen, but then he didn't have as rigidly organized clout as the others. He was released when the Food and Drug Administration, at unanimous industrial urging, lowered the safety standards for certain products. Since violation of certain safety standards figured in Harold's conviction, his attorney convinced the board of pardons that he should not be kept in jail because the standards he violated now didn't exist. No mention was made of the bribery, extortion, price-fixing, fraud and other charges which had also been part of his conviction. Harold's attorneys did point out he was a candidate for the presidency of the New York Chamber of Commerce and claimed that this would be a rehabilitative factor leading to a successful parole.

Phillip Valentine was pardoned by a governor grateful for his work in stopping a crippling strike by laborers, janitors and maids at the capitol complex. It seems no one knew who or what induced the employees to strike in the first place or what they were striking for, but "call me Phil" was able to get

137

to the root of the problem and settle the strike, thus allowing government to function freely once more. It seemed a minor reward to pardon a man who could deliver such a service to the state.

John H1 and JohnH9 got out on a simple trade. The Tom Toms traded the authorities Newark, San Diego, Portland, Oregon, and parts of greater Los Angeles for the full and complete release of their incarcerated brethren. The trade had originally included only the parts of LA, but the federal government assessors astutely reasoned the trade wasn't worth it. Of course, the government didn't accept the validity of the Tom Toms' offer right away. But then three drum brothers the government hadn't known about proved fraternal solidarity by immolating themselves and six thousand gallons of gas stored in big tanks guarded by the Army at a supply depot in New Mexico. Such action tended to back their trade claim, even though some skeptics thought the kamikaze squad hadn't meant to make such a personal sacrifice for the Cause. I'll let Wally Kearns tell his own story.

My Lee took us to a remote ranch in northern California. I was glad Donnely came along, both because of Meredith's insistence on a chaperon and because I didn't think I could handle any pebbles Wally had to throw alone. He still is the most all-around fear-inspiring man I have ever met.

Getting into Wally Kearns' private ranch is a lot like getting into Havensbrook. The Marine Corps would have a hard time taking the ranch by storm. I saw more huge guards, dark-suited, with sunglasses and tommy guns than in six hours of gangster movies.

"Gentlemen, gentlemen," said Wally graciously as he rose from his chaise longue to greet us. "How kind of you to visit a dying man. And how fortunate, I might add."

"Dying?" said Donnely as he sat in the wicker chair and took a Coke offered by the buxom brunet butler-niece. "You look perfectly healthy to me, Wally."

The Syndicate boss smiled and white teeth contrasted nicely with tanned skin. "Ah, yes, but appearances are so deceptive, for after all, I am dying. That is a legally established

138

medical fact and the basis for the judge commuting my sentence to an extended parole in the care and custody of my loving family."

Donnely smiled. "We're all dying, Wally. Some of us are just working at it harder than others. I don't suppose the medical experts could venture an opinion as to exactly when we can expect to have to send flowers?"

Wally sighed and shrugged. "Who knows? This week, next week, next year, these things are so difficult to determine. Predictive probabilities, as you know, are so often influenced by external events which, of course, is one reason I retired here to this elaborately . . . shall we say, healthily secure home."

By this time I thought I was fairly calm. Wally's announcement must have rattled me slightly, for my voice squeaked when I said, "Did you say retired?"

Wally smiled and replied, "Yes, Jack, retired. For health reasons. Of course, I still maintain some connections with . . . my former associates and occasionally act as a consultant, but my health and inclinations are such as to forbid active employment. So, might I add, is my parole. There are some pugnacious federal officials who seem to doubt the medical evidence accepted by the judge and are waiting for signs of my return to a healthy, more active life. I hope—one of those small hopes of a dying man—to live long enough to see *them* retire disappointed.

"It is through my old connections, by the way, that I learned something which made me ask you to visit me here today. Something I think you should know in order to provide for your own very near futures.

"You may have noticed my former faithful servant Bruno is not with us today. When I decided to retire here, he sought employment elsewhere. I did not begrudge him this, for I know he is a man of action and the sedate life would bore him. I was sure former associates of mine could find him suitable work.

"By the merest of chances I happened to mention Bruno to a friend of mine from Houston who was visiting me last week. My friend informed me that he had seen Bruno in Phoenix three days earlier in the company of a man he also recognized. As you may recall, Bruno is somewhat distinctive. My Houston friend watched Bruno and his companion out of curiosity and saw them meet yet another man known to both my Houston friend and myself. My friend thought little of the matter. He mentioned it to me only by chance.

"I was curious enough to make some inquiries of my own. My preliminary inquiries were so astonishing that I decided to investigate in depth. The result of my investigation caused me to send for you gentlemen."

Donnely's voice had an edge to it that I hadn't heard since Vietnam. "We would greatly appreciate your being more specific."

Wally smiled. He likes to be asked. "Bruno's companion was our mutual acquaintance, Mr. Harold Rosale, corporate tycoon and newly elected president of the New York Chamber of Commerce. They met still another acquaintance of ours, that noted labor leader Phillip 'call me Phil' Valentine who, running under the slogan 'He's a Sweetheart,' just won an almost unanimous reelection as president of his union. My research indicates they did not get together to chat about their respective political careers."

"Please go on," Donnely said. I was too nervous to talk.

Wally sighed. Like Reginald, he was playing a character. This particular role called for him to be Dostoyevsky's dying monk advising the novices. "You probably remember, dear Donnely, your first speech to the group which became known as the consortium. In it you answered my question as to what would happen if the other members of the consortium did not wish to break up a profitable partnership with you and your Group. You wisely and honestly answered that you and your Group do not produce under pressure. I believed you. Unfortunately, for you that is, evidently Mr. Rosale and Mr. Valentine did not or now do not want to believe that.

"According to my reports they have entered into a new consortium of their own, with the sole purpose of merging

140

with your Group and its major child, Apollo Industries, Inc. They are realistic enough to know you and your people will not willingly associate with them, so they are preparing to either coerce your cooperation or neutralize you. Their idea of merger is more analogous to rape than marriage. Evidently the lure of profit further obscures other realities for them. I don't think I need be any more explicit since the reports I will give you contain reams of details, including some very interesting electronic information I acquired over the weekend. I believe you know the value of securing communications."

"Naturally," Donnely said nonchalantly, "I greatly appreciate your concern and assistance. But, as you no doubt know, our former partners, formidable though they be, are not an overpowering threat. With your kind warning, I think we will adequately handle the situation."

Nice going, Donnely, I thought. Keep up the old confidence. We have nothing to fear but etc. and two of America's meanest, nastiest, sneakiest, most powerful men and their organizations. Such consoling confidence my leader distributes. I had a flash vision of me desperately trying to climb out of our pond, frantically pushing Meredith ahead of me. My vision showed little hope.

"Of your competence in such an affair I have no doubt," good old Wally replied smoothly. "But, unfortunately, my information indicates you have more than Messrs. Rosale and Valentine to worry about."

The rivers of sweat which had been running down my sides suddenly froze. The chill did little to help my nervous nausea.

"Have you ever," continued Wally, "heard of *Gabin?*"

Donnely's calm demeanor slipped for just a second and the look on his face jarred me more than any physical blow I've ever received. I had never heard of anything called Gabin, and judging from the hushed tones of my companions, I never wanted to. But I couldn't plug my ears. I could only sit and stare numbly.

"Rumors," Donnely said softly, "vague mutterings, whis-

141

pers in dark places, never anything concrete. Stories and legends. Given The Plan, I naturally tried to discover what truth lay behind the reports, but I met with no success. I eventually concluded Gabin was either a fanciful fabrication or no longer operational."

"Gabin is neither," Wally pronounced flatly. "He is alive, well, active and as competent as any legend you may have heard. It cost Valentine and Rosale a good deal to find him and even more for them to retain him. But retain him they have, as a special 'consultant and facilitator.' While Rosale and Valentine overestimate themselves they only slightly underestimate you and your Group. They know they might need the best help they can get. Since I am not available for partnership, they sought Gabin. Unfortunately for you, they found him."

Donnely frowned, one of the few times I've ever seen him with that expression.

"There are, however," said Wally in a lighter tone, "two very important points which, coupled with your intelligence and expertise, should help you with your predicament.

"*One.* Rosale and Valentine do not trust Gabin. They have hired him as an assistant, not brought him in as a partner. The distinction is lost on none of them. Gabin's contract assigns him to handle those contingencies Rosale and Valentine do not feel equipped to manage, as well as for him to give them what is termed 'final, backup, termination contingency efforts.' I need not elaborate on the meaning of that clause. My information leads me to conclude that our two former partners are carefully restricting the parameters within which they ask Gabin to operate. They also are selective about the information they share with him. In view of Gabin's honest and well-deserved reputation, Rosale and Valentine are foolish not to trust him and stupid not to turn over their entire operation to him. Their actions border on duplicity and with Gabin duplicity equals suicide.

"*Two.* Rosale and Valentine are greedy, too greedy, which is why they are attempting this operation in the first place. I do not think I need elaborate on the pitfalls of overzealous

142

greed versus excited but well-tempered ambition, not to you.

"In any event, I think these two points, plus the information I will give you before you go and the data I will forward to you as I receive it, will be of some small use."

"The use and value of your assistance are too large to adequately describe," replied Donnely. A smile replaced his frown and for some irrational reason I felt better, too. "This kind assistance you have given us is extremely interesting and of course invaluable," continued Donnely thoughtfully. "We are grateful. But something bothers me, something, I might add, which is very influential in my evaluation of your information. Exactly why are you telling us all this?"

Wally, the Dying Kindly Old Uncle, smiled and for a brief flash he was Wild Wally of ice-pick, pineapple and machine-gun fame once more. "You mean, Daniel, that you can't believe me until you figure out why I'm helping you and what's in it for me, right?"

Donnely smiled back while I trembled some more. "Right."

The kindly uncle returned. "Oh, there are many reasons, my boy, many reasons. For example, some of my former business associates have expressed slight concern over this new group. My former associates aren't sure it will be good for the business community as a whole for this new consortium to become overly solvent. It might become too sloppy and/or too solvent. Mind you, my former associates are not concerned enough to actively oppose the new consortium. If they were that concerned, there would be no point in my calling you here, or there would be no new consortium."

Yeah, I thought, and no Harold Rosale or Phil Valentine.

"But really, Mr. Donnely," continued Wally in an almost piqued tone, "you should not have too much trouble understanding my motivation. True, your interests do parallel those of my associates . . . I mean my *former* associates, but of course, my real reasons for helping you are purely personal.

"If you remember correctly, I was greatly impressed by the extraordinary creativity of you and your Group. I still am. I think such genius deserves to prosper and I enjoy aiding it

143

whenever I can. Without such people as you, Mr. Mason and the others in your Group, life in these modern times of heavy organization, sterile plastic and bland life-styles would be dreary indeed. Besides, I have no love for either Mr. Rosale or Mr. Valentine and if I can help you and your Group, I can aid genius, establish an interesting contest which might otherwise be a sad defeat and do some old friends a good turn. What better motivation could a man have?"

How's that for an explanation of a probable pebble-to-pond thrower?

Donnely smiled."Wally, I believe you, and once again, on behalf of The Group, thank you. Now you said you had some more details you would like to give us . . . ?"

The Plan

Larry claims only a handful of technicians could have installed the bugs and the camera and that the whole system must have cost Wally and his "former associates" a small fortune. I didn't care about the technical details; it was the result flickering on the screen which frightened me.

You've seen it before. In special dollar-a-head neighborhood movie theaters far from the normal theater section of town where you sit with motley dressed crowds of cinema buffs. Or on nights when the world and sleeping don't seem to jibe with your reality and the only thing left is the boob tube's display of 1937–1967 movies. The film print is old; the sound track is scratchy. The characters live through shades of gray, an intensity somehow more real than modern flesh-and-blood color. Their words fade in and out of the sound track. The features have fuzzed with time and tenuous technique. But you're right there with them, the villains. It's the big meeting scene.

Harold Rosale looked even more dapper in the movies than I remembered him. Of course, I seldom saw him in anything other than his custom-cut prison blues. There he was, casually lolling on a sofa in the small, ornately furnished upstairs salon of the very private New York brothel, a slightly overaged dandy with cigarette held daintily in his finely manicured fingers. Phil "Sweetheart" Valentine's leathery toughness took on a strange kind of stringiness when recorded by the camera, an emaciated bull in a gaudy china shop. Their voices even sounded different.

"Relax," Chamber of Commerce President Rosale said

classically, probably unaware of his role. "He'll be here soon and he's nothing we can't handle."

"I just don't like it," replied Valentine. His tone wasn't worried, but it was far from happy. "We may need his help, but we gotta be very careful when it comes time and place to cut him off. I know he don't like us holding him instead of him running his own show. I don't care what anybody says, I still don't trust him. I wouldn't trust him even if we were being square with him."

"Which is precisely," countered Rosale carefully, "why we are not being square with him. That, and I see no need for anyone else to share in our venture. Gabin is our security blanket. Anything we get into and can't handle, he can. Additionally, we are so busy being careful to cheat and control him, we have to trust ourselves. Neither of us has to worry about getting screwed by the other."

Both men looked at each other and smiled. On cue (actually, Meredith cut out the next sequence of three empty minutes from Wally's unedited footage and spliced the film together so it flowed) the door opened and *he* entered.

I tell Meredith that if one picture is worth a thousand words, a movie or a part of a movie is worth more than a whole novel. The little screen in Apollo's projection room showed Valentine and Rosale, two of the most powerful men in the world, standing to face the visitor. Their actions and faces clearly told what they felt: fear and respect.

The visitor in the movie is tall but not overly tall. After studying the one blurred photograph and the small bit of film, Reginald and Donnely put his natural height at six two. He is thin, for while a thin man can use padding to add bulk to his appearance, girdles can only contain bulk, they cannot conceal it. In the photograph, the movie and our eventual brief encounters, he was thin: thin like a rapier, hard like a saber. I've never seen him with other than brownish blond hair and sallow Gallic features. His voice is flat, unemotional. In the movie he wore a trench coat and kept his hands suspiciously in his pockets.

"It's good to see you again, Mr. Gabin," said Rosale softly,

146

politely, his sharp confidence dulled with anticipation and respect.

"Really?" asked the visitor.

As the three men on the screen talked, I kept flashing back to the first briefing Donnely gave The Group on Phase III. At that time all we had on Gabin was what Donnely knew and a blurred photograph of a man sitting by himself in an outdoor Paris café, calmly, inoffensively reading a newspaper. Donnely stood in front of the screen and talked to us. The man's picture looked out at us from the screen, the image blown up until the grains in the photograph almost blurred what little clarity the picture possessed. I could hear Donnely's words from the briefing as if they were spliced between the dialogue in the movie:

"In the real worlds of the borderlines of our society there exist very few of the characters who proliferate in fiction," Donnely had said. *"The world of crime and related areas knows few true geniuses. The Gamesman, an old Armenian gentleman living in Brooklyn, is one. He is virtually retired. There is a woman operating in Las Vegas whose work leads me to believe she will soon join the ranks of acknowledged masters. Sui Ling of Hong Kong recently proved once again, as if such proof were needed, that he too is a master of the art. There is a man in Paris, another in London, a woman in Rome, two twins whose genius operates in tandem working out of Turkey, a remarkable boy operating in Prague and some others who are scattered through Africa and South America who may someday show their merit. Our friend Wally Kearns is close to this level, although I think he rightly questions his ultimate ability. From some of these people, from vague whispers I heard in the street, from strange events curiously woven together, I learned of this man, the man on the screen, the man who I had hoped was only a legend or whose reputation was at least overblown, Gabin."*

"Isn't this a peculiar meeting place?" asked Gabin of his fellow cinema apparitions.

"Most true criminal geniuses share at least one common trait besides their genius: desire for anonymity. But even in the unrecorded vague volumes of knowledge concerning their world, little information exists on Victor Gabin. I tend to believe the part of the legend

147

that says he grew up in a circus. I do know he trained for his career in the military. Gabin served with the Special Forces in the early days of the Southeast Asian war. He obviously drained them dry of all the knowledge and experience they could give him. He supposedly arranged for the Army to grant him a two-year educational leave at MIT, studying what we have no way of knowing. He next spent some time in the Pentagon, working in their computer complex. One day he simply disappeared."

"It seems like a good enough place to me," said Phil Valentine a good deal more kindly than he would to anyone else.

"Is it safe to talk here?" countered Gabin.

"Naturally, the Army worried about him. When they went looking, they found the first known overt act of his genius. He programmed the government computers to order our clandestine services to destroy his identity. All records relating to Gabin vanished. Even records of the destruction were either skillfully buried in computer bureaucracy or themselves destroyed. I have a feeling Gabin had been planning this move for years, probably since his boyhood, so there wasn't much to destroy: he would have remembered what little there was. We have no idea who he really is, where he was born, nothing. All service records, files, photographs are gone. By the time the Army realized all this any people who might have known more about him were scattered to the four winds. Gabin thus became a unique individual: He is anyman. A well-trained, brilliant anyman. The Army did, however, find evidence of what may have been his second overt act of genius. The accounts of the Special Forces black money, the money they use for bribes and other such miscellaneous expenses, came up short. Exactly how short the Army isn't sure, partially because of their own sloppiness and partially because of Gabin's fine work. But the scanty records show our boy might have made off with around one million dollars."

"Safe?" exclaimed Rosale indignantly. "Of course it's safe to talk here! I own a major portion of this establishment!"

Gabin smiled, almost as if he knew Wally Kearns owned *the* major portion. "Nevertheless, you will not be offended if I am less than explicit. Tape recorders operate in the most unusual places."

"Gabin is a true artist. His satisfaction comes as much from

working as from the fruits of his labor. He developed a very clever way of operating. He pulled a few minor jobs to build his reputation. He put the word out in the right circles that he existed and he gave himself a name. Now the jobs come to him. He still does projects on his own, but because his isolation presents an operational intelligence problem, he mostly does consultant or contract work. You put out the word in the right places that you have a problem and a price. The size of the price tells Gabin the scope of the problem and helps him decide if he's interested. He contacts you. He runs the show. It must have cost Rosale and Valentine a fortune to get him to work their way."

"You realize, of course," said Gabin, "that my fee will be paid in full regardless of whether you actually do decide to give me work."

"Of course," murmured Rosale, "of course."

"Gabin's clients come from everywhere there is money, power, greed and fear. He has worked for private individuals and industry. He did two jobs for the U.S. government. This picture was taken by a CIA agent on Gabin's last government job. Gabin found out about the photograph shortly before the agent vanished, but by then it was too late; the photo had gone to Washington. Evidently Gabin hasn't considered it worth his effort to destroy all the copies. Gabin once worked for Wally Kearns. A very young, very smart, very tough group of newcomers were slowly taking New York away from Wally and his 'former' associates. Wally and his boys tried everything they could think of. All their efforts met defeat. They hired Gabin. Four days later the controlling coterie of the new group died when the town house they were meeting in suddenly exploded. The police quite honestly deduced that a group of left-wing radicals had accidentally destroyed themselves while making bombs. Wally and the boys had no more trouble with those competitors."

"As I understand it, you have nothing for me now, but you may wish me to see to former associates of yours and to be so prepared."

"You got it," replied the noted labor leader.

"Legend gives Gabin some quirks which I think we can depend on. He has an artist's soul. He likes things done right, with precision and taste. He is a loner, both in nature and activity, although

149

he may use unwitting accomplices. While he is adventuresome, he likes tried-and-true simple methods more than complicated, cumbersome schemes. Not that he is against complexity: just needless, cosmetic waste. Above all, he is honest and trustworthy. He even goes so far as to guarantee never to work against a former client. My mistake, and I must apologize to The Group for it, is that I did not pursue the legend enough to find the reality. If I had done so, I would have hired Gabin for a trivial task, and we would now be safe from him as former clients. Our predicament with the Messrs. Rosale and Valentine is considerably compounded by the fact that Gabin is the best."

"I do not particularly enjoy the terms of our association," Gabin calmly stated. "If not for the compensation, I would not have taken you on as clients. The challenge I so far see is to keep awake waiting to be needed. You lack the aesthetic appreciation of most of my clients. You have hired me as a waiting consultant for six months. I hope whatever business you are transacting will take no longer, for at the end of six months, you will see me no more. As I mentioned earlier, my methods—when you give me the word—will be my own. Since you tell me little of the *why*, I will tell you nothing of the *how*. I am sure that legally you are just as happy not to know. Ethically and artistically, I always work this way. Always. Your strange decision to be, shall we say, less than candid has not affected that at all, though if I were different, it certainly would. And now, good evening, *gentlemen*."

My concentration broke when the film switched to scenes of Rosale and Valentine in various stages of debauchery. I suddenly felt Donnely beside me. The two of us sat there, watching images flicker briefly on the screen; then the clip ended and the darkness of the auditorium covered us.

"Does he worry you, Jack?" asked Donnely softly, a voice I could hear but not see.

I didn't know how to answer Donnely. I wasn't sure what he was asking. "Of course. But we have no choice. We already decided that."

"I want you to remember one thing, Jack. Everything will be OK. The Plan will take care of all of us, of you and Meredith. We can handle Gabin just like we can handle the others.

Just remember to follow The Plan. And go with the flow, Jack, ride the ripples. When something happens you're not sure of, go with the flow."

Just then the flow seemed to be for me to leave Donnely and go back to work. I often think of him as I left him that afternoon, sitting in the dark, alone except for his thoughts of us and The Plan.

I should take some time to explain the effect Wally's news had on the rest of The Group. Donnely arranged for all of us to meet secretly at the G. Orevidal residence two days after our conference with Wally. Donnely didn't leave a thing out of his briefing. He told us The Plan provided three options for our present predicament. The first one was to ignore things and let nature take its course, looking only to immediate survival. The second one was to sell out immediately and disappear to a secure hideaway. The third was to fight back. He told us the only one which offered better than a fifty–fifty chance of secure survival was Number 2.

Raoul spoke for The Group, but he didn't know that until after he had finished his speech. He turned down his transistor radio, stood up and addressed everyone, although he faced Donnely, who stood on the stage at the front of the small auditorium.

"I look at it this way," Raoul said, his voice tight with emotion. "We've all been through a lot together and we all worked and risked everything to get something and do something we never had or did before. Donnely showed us The Plan and we helped him pull it of. Not many people get a chance like that and something like what we've done sort of binds us together, for better or worse as they say. The Group is like family to me. We are what we do and we have to live with that no matter what happens. I don't like the idea of getting iced, but I also don't like the idea of living cold either. I don't mind losing Apollo, but I don't want those creeps to have it. I also don't like the idea of letting them decide for me that it's time I moved on and retired or hid. I say let's fight them. I'm not worried. After all, what have they got? We got The Plan and each other."

One by one the others said they agreed, including Meredith and me. I knew Donnely was trying hard not to cry, mainly because I was too.

Besides the reasons Raoul gave, I think there was one more thing which made The Group decide to fight: We were bored with being corporate executives. We wanted a challenge. In a way, maybe it was a healthy thing for The Group that somebody threw the Rosale-Valentine pebble into our pond.

One of the hardest things I had to do in the next few weeks was to lose consistently at chess to my secretary, Edward. Not that I'm a particularly good chess player, although I have improved considerably since the first time Donnely and I faced each other across a board in prison (I lost in eight moves), or that Edward is a particularly good player (I beat him regularly before this stage of The Plan); it's just that we were both trying so hard to lose I had to be twice the player I normally am. What with all the rest that was on my mind, I really had to work at concentrating hard enough to succeed in losing.

Why, you may ask, was I wasting time and effort playing chess with secretary Edward at all, let alone trying to lose to him? And why was he trying to lose to me? The answer is simple: Edward Arlington Kaufman III was a traitor in the employ of the Rosale-Valentine consortium. I had to lose at chess to him, so I could gain his confidence as a defeated opponent confessing to the victor and he had to lose to me in order to gain my confidence as a nice but dim-witted underling in whom it would be safe to confide.

We thought it would be better to play it our way.

Edward's treachery was only one of many things Wally's "former associates" uncovered. It seems Edward had been compromised by the paltry offer of a ten-thousand-dollar Judas fee and a forty percent increase in salary, plus executive status, once the coup was complete. I think he could have held out for more because Rosale and Valentine must have known we would have paid him a good deal more than that to reward loyalty. It just goes to show you how cheaply you can buy Ivy-covered souls.

The basic plan uncovered by Wally's "former associates"

was simple. Rosale and Valentine had formed an investment company-consortium called Sebek, Inc. For those of you, like me, who didn't echo Donnely's ejaculation of "Of course!" when you learned the Rosale-Valentine consortium name, let me enlighten you. The reference book in the G. Orevidal library says Sebek is an Egyptian deity of evil. Sebek is usually depicted with a crocodile head, representing the destructive power of the sun. I had no idea that Rosale and Valentine were that imaginative. I actually think they just strung some letters together and the whole name thing is coincidence. Donnely says that if that is true, then coincidence sure tosses some funny pebbles in some appropriate ponds.

Sebek, Inc., was investing heavily in any and all companies connected with Apollo Industries, Inc., including buying shares of the mother company itself. Sebek also had a large pool of cash on hand waiting to pick up shares of Apollo and related industries as they became available after the "Apollo Panic."

By controlling as many of the service and other companies linked to Apollo as they could, Rosale and Valentine hoped to use Sebek's power to complement the push coming from Valentine's union. Valentine and his associates controlled only a small portion of workers in Apollo and Apollo-related industries, but through the use of picket lines, legitimate influence and their standard persuasive techniques, "Call me Phil the Sweetheart" and the boys were sure they could at least slow Apollo's firm walk to a sick, sluggish crawl. This, coupled with pressure exerted by Rosale Industries and Sebek, Inc., in the business world and their lackeys in government, could cause what they called their Apollo Panic. In the panic, they hoped to use stock-buying techniques to gain "legitimate" control over most of Apollo as we liquidated part of our assets to find the funds to fight the symptoms of their work. Rosale and Valentine would use Gabin to grab what they couldn't through their own efforts and to "provide" for The Group if necessary.

We started work on The Plan the day Donnely briefed The Group. Disguised and well equipped, we fanned out over the

153

country, acquiring the materials we would need for our fight. The G. Orevidal residence served as our base.

Donnely rigged a schedule so that two of us were always at the Arizona Apollo home plant "working" as "normal" so that Sebek wouldn't get suspicious. Donnely also stationed one of us in disguise in Hamilton to act as a backup in case the overt team got into trouble. For the first two weeks of this phase we relied heavily on Wally's benevolence. He didn't tell us what to do or give us any hints; that would have been too much for him. But he answered our questions and supplied us with as much of the necessary information as he could. For instance, he helped us find the right phones to tap. We didn't have the resources even to contemplate general oversight of Sebek and company, but Wally's boys knew the key points in each of Sebek's components and with that knowledge we found the key pressure points in mother Sebek. At the end of two weeks we could have helped Wally, had he been interested in anything we could give him.

The basic idea of The Plan in this phase was to gain control of Sebek, then use that control to make Sebek defeat itself. Simple, right? Well, simple in theory, profoundly complex underneath.

Donnely picked Chicago for the major combat zone. Although I think Donnely could have structured The Plan so The Group could have done it alone, he thought it safe and necessary to bring in outside assistance. Unlike the bank job when we pulled in Chief Parker and Officer Hodgson (with his riot gun) as unknowing outside assistance, Donnely decided some of our outside assistance should be at least partially aware and experienced. Of course, we already had Wally Kearns, who, as an interested nonneutral observer and sometimes assistant, was a fairly knowledgeable participant, but Donnely didn't tell him what we were doing. That was OK with Wally; he found it more fun to try to figure it out for himself.

At this point I think it appropriate and necessary to answer a question some of you might have: Where were John H1 and his drum brothers? Why weren't they involved in Sebek?

154

What were they doing, and what *really* happened to them? The basic answer to these questions is that we again pulled the drum brothers into The Plan.

The Sebek associates were wary of the drum brothers mainly because they weren't sure they could control them. Donnely thinks that Rosale and Valentine were also too stupid to figure out how the Tom Toms could be of any assistance to Sebek. That was a major mistake on their part, for the Tom Toms hadn't forgotten Valentine, Rosale or any of their other former business partners.

Destroying the world in order to save it is an expensive business. Just look at how much an atom bomb costs or how much it takes to maintain a battalion of Marines. It's no less expensive for a private group with a large hate and a love of their ideal. The million dollars acquired by the Brotherhood through their work for the original consortium was almost gone by this time and they were looking for ways to replenish their coffers and carry on with the crusade. Most of the methods they tried on their own were miserable failures. They were too devoted to hating to have time for anything else. So they were beginning to look toward us, their old associates, for their "just dues." From what Wally had heard third-hand, the drum brothers weren't going to come asking. That was one reason he "retired" to his California fortress. I thought Donnely had flipped when he told me we were going to use the Tom Toms for The Plan. He almost lost my confidence when he told me how.

Throughout this phase of The Plan, Donnely's chief concern was Gabin. Donnely didn't want to face Gabin until the proper moment and a major portion of The Plan was designed to ensure the auspicious arrival of the proper moment. That's what we were working on that dreadful afternoon in Gary, Indiana.

I didn't like it at all. Not at all. The longer I lay underneath the brick outcropping on the roof of the tenement, the less I liked it. I didn't mind the physical discomfort, the cramped muscles, the soreness from lying on jagged rocks or the eyestrain from peering through binoculars for more than an hour without a break. But the mental strain of watching Meredith, the woman with whom I had already decided to spend the rest of my life, sitting by the picture window inside the grimy restaurant across that dark-even-in-daylight Gary street almost killed me.

Reginald surpassed himself with the makeup job he did on Meredith. I barely recognized her. She was the most pregnant poverty-stricken woman I have ever seen. He schooled her so long and so well that the bitterness on her pouty, paunchy, cheek-pad face hid her loving nature from everyone but her friends. John H9 was never very observant, but Donnely didn't need my urging to take as few chances as necessary when he sent Meredith to meet him.

The rendezvous lasted fifteen of the longest minutes of my life. While I watched from the roof, I could hear the conversation from the bug Larry planted at the table.

". . . so he got a little handy with you, knocked you around a little, fired you and blacklisted you with all the unions and major companies. So what does that got to do with us?" John H9's words did not exactly drip with sympathy after hearing Meredith's bitterly related tale, but he did appear to believe it.

"Maybe nothing," replied Meredith in a snotty voice I've asked her never to use in my presence, "maybe lots. My friend Sarah says you Tom Toms are the baddest dudes around. Maybe so, maybe not. I can't say for sure. I only heard about you from her. And that mother Rosale."

"What he have to say about us? Come on, lady, come across." John H9 leaned menacingly across the table. I must confess I really wanted my Marine rifle at that moment. I grow very ashamed when I think how ugly I felt then.

"Not much. An' he never told me nothin'. Nothin' direct, mind you. The day he moved me out of the typing pool to be one of his 'special secretaries' he was showing this cat named Ballentine or Valentine around and they were talking about brothers. I guess seeing me kind of brought up the subject, and they lump you guys and all blacks together. Anyways, they laughed when they saw me and said something like,

156

'Too bad those stupid Tom Toms don't take women. We'd have to worry about her'—meanin' me—''bout her tellin' them we were going to make millions by movin' in on Donnely and crew.' Then they laughed some more. Next day that mother Rosale had me transferred to his special pool. You know the rest."

John H9 leaned back in the booth and I relaxed slightly. He looked across at who he thought was Judy Marks. He didn't know that the real Judy Marks, who had worked for Rosale's firm in a manner similar to the story Meredith told, was winging her way to Paris on a six-month all-expense-paid vacation. John H9 smiled, playing the crafty criminal he had studied so carefully in the tough guy movies. "So what? What's all this got to do with us?"

"You guys are supposed to be real hot. Well, here's your chance. Rosale is pulling something he don't want you guys into and you got a chance to make some money if you move on him."

"Why would you want us to do that?"

"I want that mother dead. I figure you'll have to kill him, the way he and you Tom Toms work."

John H9 smiled. "You think you gonna get some coin out of this?"

"I ain't that dumb. You wouldn't give me the sweat off your back. I figure there's no money in it for me, but I sure as hell want Rosale's ass in the sling. And you guys can do it for me. After this I've done all I can. I'm splitting, and ain't nobody in this place gonna hear from me again."

John H9 slid out from behind the table. He swayed slightly as he stood looking down on Judy Marks, moving slowly as if dancing to a deep martial melody heard only by him. I wondered how many hours a day he spent practicing his cool. His parting words dripped with contempt as he smiled sweetly. "Maybe we've got somethin', baby. Maybe." Then he sauntered out.

Two days later one of noted labor leader Phil Valentine's runners made his morning call at a Chicago employment center to pick up "consideration fees" from those few men in

157

the shuffling mass who could still afford to bribe someone for a job. If one of the unemployed didn't have enough ready cash to make a respectable contribution, he could always walk two blocks and borrow the money at forty-eight percent interest from a lone shark affiliated with Wally Kearns' "former associates." One of the men who approached the runner obviously didn't have the cash, nor did he look strong enough to hold a job and thus warrant a floating kickback agreement. I don't know how Reginald manages to shrivel to the emaciated wino stage, but then I've never been able to figure out how Bogart made his rugged ugly face twinkle.

"Hey, hey, mister," stuttered Reginald as he picked at the runner's sleeve, "I ain't got no money and, hell, I barely can stand up, let alone hold a job. But I figure if I tell you what I heard, maybe Mr. Valentine would see clear to let you spring a few bucks for me so's I can get some good wine, maybe a burger."

Normally the runner dealt with bums, beggars and freeloaders like a dog shedding fleas, but something about the wino's character, some forcefulness made the runner bend closer to the rancid old man. Besides, while most of the street people knew about his boss' employment service racket, very, very few people dared menton Phil the Sweetheart by name. "What are you talking about, old man?"

"Well, you know the elevated train terminal on Michigan Street? The part where it's nice and dry and you can step in out of the wind and the cops won't hassle you to move along for at least fifteen minutes? Anyways, I's biding my time there yesterday, wondering if my broker would come through, when I heard 'bout Mr. Valentine."

After a few very impatient seconds the runner demanded, "Well? What did you hear?"

"'Bout how them musicians fellows were looking for him. Don't know what Mr. Rosale wants with a bunch of musicians, but they can't quite seem to latch onto whatever it is he's doing, and I figure Mr. Valentine will be right happy to know that he can most likely meet up with his friends if he just stands and waits in the windbreak at the El station. Most likely the cops won't bother him none, no, sir."

158

"What the hell are you talking about? What musicians?"

"Them drummers, that there whole band of 'em I heard talking as they got off the El trains. You know, they call themselves the Tom Toms. Sort of a silly name for a band, if you ask me, but what the hell, if they're looking for Mr. Valentine and he hired them, they can't be all bad."

"Look," said the runner, his curiosity fighting with his impatience, "just what exactly did you hear? Tell me the words they said, old man, tell me the words."

Reginald wrinkled his brow. He pursed his lips and touched them with his fingers. He strained his memory. "You know, it's right there, right on the tip of my head, but it's kind of hard for it to come out. Most likely that's because I'm so thirsty and so hungry. It seems like ages since I had me anything decent for sustenance, since the nectar of the gods passed these old, dry lips. Why, my memory is just plumb pooped out from hunger and thirst. Now I suppose it could be. . . ."

The runner used one meaty paw to stuff a bill in the wino's torn pocket. With the other he grabbed the wino's grimy collar and pulled him close. "That's a fiver," hissed the runner, "enough for you to buy heaven at the McDonald's and the liquor store up the street. It's also enough for cab fare to St. Luke's emergency ward, which is what you'll need to use it for if you don't cut this crap and tell me what you got to say."

"Amazin'," murmured the wino quickly, "simply amazin'. My memory has returned unimpaired. the power of proper persuasion. Picture three very big, very tough-looking black men, one of them obviously carrying a firearm of some sort barely concealed beneath his jacket as they walk past my humble resting spot. One says to the other—and mind you, the disrespect is his, all his—he says, 'That mother Valentine is gonna have one big surprise when the Tom Toms move in on his little takeover.' And one of the other gentlemen says, 'And John H1 says us drum brothers might even get to waste those crazies, too.' Then, I fear, they passed out of my old ears' range. Not, however, before I remembered that famous slogan of my youth, 'Loose lips sink ships!' "

The runner grunted. "You remember that, Pops. You re-

159

member that real good. Nothing about this goes anywhere else. Now get lost." The runner pushed him away. The union man paid no attention as his most recent acquaintance eagerly shuffled through the doors, past the McDonald's, and vanished.

The runner stroked his chin for several seconds; then, just as we had gambled, he walked to the pay phone booth. Seconds later he connected with his overseer and the runner's voice came through our monitor loud and clear as he said, "I think I've got something Sweetheart Phil should know."

"We must account for the potential impact of forceful random factors or The Plan will be jeopardized," Donnely told us in the first briefing. "By far the two most important such factors are Gabin and the Tom Toms. Both exist within our set sphere of operation and both must be accounted for. The most obvious way to account for them is to let them cancel each other out. By their very erratic, irrationally effective, volatile nature, the Tom Toms constitute a dangerous force bordering on the insurmountable. If we prick their already excited potential toward Sebek, our friends Rosale and Valentine will have no choice but to counter the Tom Toms' threat with an equal, if not greater, force. Our former associates are astute enough to realize the only such force they have at their disposal is Gabin. If all goes according to The Plan, Gabin and the Tom Toms will keep occupied with their own conflict long enough for The Plan to neutralize and defeat the main threat posed by Sebek."

Three days after Reginald's alcoholic performance we intercepted a phone call between Valentine in Chicago and Rosale in Phoenix: The two free market moguls agreed that their very special consultant needed to be assigned to their newly discovered problem. That afternoon two drum brothers in Chicago "accidentally" drowned in the same bathtub and their brethren vanished into grieving seclusion.

It took thirty-seven days to prepare for the operational stage of The Plan. On the surface, we kept up the pretense of business as usual at Apollo in Arizona. With two of us always conspicuously present at the company headquarters and our

160

erratic life-styles, Rosale and Valentine never guessed we knew. If they did, they concealed their knowledge far better than we did ours. Our intelligence and Wally's sources indicated Sebek's plans were progressing as before.

Donnely stuck with his old policy of keeping me pretty much in the dark about the exact details of The Plan, which shows his grasp on reality. Had I known exactly how he was using me, I would probably have blown the whole thing. When I was actively working on The Plan (even when all I was doing was maintaining my Arizona cover), I really thought I was doing what I was doing. What I was doing was fairly simple.

We needed a good deal of material and preparation. I spent a lot of time flying around the country acquiring everything from costumes to 9mm Ingram machine pistols, arranging everything from false passports to escape plans disguised as vacation cruises for phony credit union travel groups. Part of Donnely's reason for having me do this was the preparations really had to be made, part of his reason was to keep me busy, and part of his reason you'll learn later. I used my identity as an Apollo executive checking the market situation to cover the majority of these trips. Hints I dropped to Edward, my secretary, and carefully rehearsed behavior around the office helped cover me on the rest of the trips, those trips when my role as a corporate official just wouldn't wash. On those trips I simply disappeared. My cover for the disappearances was founded in our knowledge of Rosale and Valentine's beliefs. They always viewed life with the half wisdom of a greedy, obnoxious cynic. It came as no surprise to them that my relationship with Meredith (which we knew they knew about) was "souring" and that my disappearances were really erotic forays in which I "got a little on the side."

Donnely told me that one of the easiest ways to fool quasi-critical cynics is to supply them with proof of their wisdom.

I spent most of my foray time helping with the fake Chicago headquarters. Donnely and the Professor found a huge abandoned factory just over the Chicago line into Gary.

161

They set up three pounds of phony paperwork corporate structure to hide our acquisition of the building and the day the old Italian gentleman "Signatio Marchetti" (admirably played by Reginald) signed the papers, the covert construction team moved in. We poured over two million dollars in carefully laundered funds into that factory. I was gone for part of the construction phase, occupied with my forays and my stints at Arizona Apollo headquarters. On day 37, Larry, Alfred, Donnely and I spread our fingerprints through the factory. Donnely told me we did that in case someone with a little clever wisdom and skill wanted to check and see if we actually used the building.

The factory was a four-story structure. The top floor had been the company's offices. Donnely redesigned the office level into a miniature version of our living quarters at the G. Orevidal residence, the "real" Chicago headquarters. He even had the Professor stock the tiny greenhouse on the roof with his least favorite plants. I remember Donnely murmuring something to the Professor about us all having to make sacrifices, but it didn't mean anything to me at the time. One vast room took up the bottom three floors of the old factory. Donnely had it renovated to look like a regular warehouse. After all the goods were distributed, Donnely had Larry blow dust through the air conditioning-heating system. When Larry finished, it looked as if the merchandise had been sitting in the warehouse for months.

"I don't get it," I asked Donnely as we moved into the fake briefing room, carefully touching everything we would logically touch if the room had been real. "It doesn't follow. Downstairs we've stashed all that stuff in a 'warehouse.' Upstairs it looks like we live here. Given that stuff, it just doesn't logically connect. It's like two contradictory chemicals in the same formula."

Donnely looked at me with surprise and, I think, some admiration. He also looked a little worried, as if maybe he were upset because my reasoning process was improving. "Very good, Jack. Very good indeed.

"But you're forgetting a very fundamental principle of human knowledge. The same entity can and usually is different things to different people. Take any two people to the Art Institute or, better yet, take them downtown and show them the Picasso statue. One person will look at it as disgusting, an ugly waste of money. Another will find in it the very essence of art. Voltaire used this in *Candide*. What we've done here is help that quirk of reality and bend the result to fit The Plan.

"You already know how Sebek fits into the warehouse. We needed it for them. But we are facing more than Sebek. We have Gabin and the Tom Toms. Although I doubt it, the Tom Toms may overlook us. Gabin has not forgotten that we, not the drum brothers, are his potentially major commitment. If he is true to his past and to logic, he will come after us en masse. He will hunt us in our hole, hit us where and when we feel safest. Where would that be?"

"In our G. Orevidal residence," I replied without hesitation. "That's why we built it, or at least partially why. Next to the catastrophe survival centers, it's the safest, most secure place we have."

"Precisely. Gabin knows we're smart enough to know we need a safe, secure place. And he'll look for it. Because he's busy with the drum brothers, he won't be able to devote his full efforts to the search, but given time, he would find the real G. Orevidal residence and he would find us. That would mean disaster, ultimate, bloody disaster."

Donnely could have glossed over that part and I wouldn't have minded.

"So what we do," continued Donnely, "is provide Gabin with what he is looking for: our rathole, our bastion and, as he would see it, our Maginot Line."

"That's why you had Larry and Alfred build in the security system," I said excitedly. "The TV cameras, the hidden sleeping gas jets, the special things. That's why you used that elaborate subcontracting system. Not only did you want to hide the phony warehouse's real owners, you wanted to hide the phony hideout's real owners, just like you hid the real

163

owners of the real G. Orevidal residence! And by doing both the fakes in the same building, you cheaply uncomplicate matters! Right?"

"Right. When Gabin finds this, as I'm sure he soon will, he finds us with a dummy warehouse. He'll see the warehouse is just that, a dummy warehouse designed to mask our rathole. Of course, he won't tell Rosale and Valentine what he's found, so they will find only the warehouse."

By then I was really excited. "That's why when I come here you haven't had me do all the careful things to avoid detection you taught me, right? You figure somehow Gabin will find this place through me, and deduce what we want him to, right?"

"Right."

"One thing bothers me," I said after a moment's reflection. "If Gabin is as good as you say he is, we can't fool him for long. He's whittled the Tom Toms down to about two dozen members in this area and another dozen scattered across the country. At that rate he'll be through with them soon; then he's free to take us on whenever Rosale and Valentine give him the word. In a way that will be good for us, because he'll have taken care of the Tom Toms. But it won't take Gabin long to tumble on to the fact that this place, as good as it is, is a phony, that we don't really live here. I know everyone stays here a lot, but that man is no dummy. He'll find out."

"By that time," Donnely lied to me, "he won't have any employers to ask him to execute his contract. We will have pulled the scam on Sebek by then and there will be no point in him pursuing the matter."

"Oh," I said. Donnely's logic fell into place, but even then I felt something was wrong. I went over it again and again in my mind. the logic kept falling into place. I didn't know then that what was bothering me was that the logic, while valid, was falling into the wrong place. and while technically Donnely lied to me, he actually wasn't sure if he had or not, so I can't really call him dishonest.

The four of us sat huddled in the dark on the roof of the tenement opposite the factory. It was a pleasant night, cool but not cold. The industrial stench seemed weaker than usual. Indeed, the sunset reflecting off the lake earlier that evening had lacked some of its normal metallic green tinge. It was just past midnight. The neighborhood was fairly quiet, the normal night sounds of the city streets were pleasantly drowned out by the strains of a radio from one of the tenement apartments. I heard the faint melody of "Duke of Earl." The music reminded me of Raoul and his ever-present radio, now on open duty in Arizona. The words in the song tell of a young man making his way in the world unimpaired because he's the Duke of Earl. The source of his strength, of his dukedom, is his duchess, his love. I thought of my lovely duchess, Meredith, and sighed. I know it's bizarre, but sitting there on that tenement roof in the most dangerous phase of The Plan, I realized how truly lucky I was.

Larry and Alfred had constructed an elaborate, yet easily portable security system of closed-circuit TV camera monitors which allowed us to view all sides of the factory from our perch. One of the Group manned that post continually from the day the final papers on the factory were signed. I think it was just a coincidence that Donnely had the four of us there that night of all nights. We were rehearsing The Plan (at least as I knew it), looking for loopholes and unforeseen contingencies, when Larry hissed at us.

Donnely postulated that anyone trying to break into the factory would concern himself with security devices designed to monitor and prevent that activity. Consequently Donnely concluded that any intruder would not discover the TV cameras concealed on the buildings surrounding the factory which let us watch our fake headquarters-warehouse. Donnely increased the odds of his assumption by unleashing the combined geniuses of Larry and Alfred in making and locating these special external cameras.

"Bingo," whispered Larry. "On the roof of the house behind the factory, just opposite us, only on the other side of the factory, the side in the shadow. At first I didn't see him, but I've got him now."

It was like watching *Mission Impossible* filmed in the days of

165

the silent screen. The hooded figure's black camouflage clothing blended into the shadows of the buildings until he was almost invisible. I know that at least some of the time Larry was using the infrared cameras. The figure flitted from shadow to shadow like Nureyev gliding across the stage, unencumbered by the knapsack on his back. The intruder crossed the street to the factory's rear at an easy run. In one hand he held what looked like a thick, flat board, while in the other he held a long pole. He ran to within two feet of the fence, dropped the board device, then jogged back to the middle of the street. He paused for a second, psyching himself as he faced the fence, his long rod extended. If he had been on horseback, he'd have been a knight preparing to impale a dragon with his lance. He charged. He pole vaulted the ten-foot, electrically charged barbed-wire-topped fence. Instead of landing on the ground in the four feet between the fence and the factory wall where pressure alarms might wait, he stopped his descent by catching trapeze-style onto a row of bricks I would have sworn a pigeon would have found narrow. While he hung there by one hand, he fitted a suction-cup device on his free hand, then put similar devices on his feet. Less than two minutes after he vaulted the fence, he scrambled to the top of the roof, avoided all the security alarms and light systems and went to work on the roof trapdoor. The three locks took him ten minutes, but then they were the best money could buy. He silently opened the door, and after a moment's inspection for hidden alarms, cameras or ambushes, he slid from sight.

"I didn't think the suction-cup devices were perfected yet," muttered Alfred absentmindedly.

"Just barely," replied Larry. "The Army has a few sets, but they aren't stable enough for long climbs."

"Two of those sets were stolen from the Fort Bragg experimental lab last week," commented Donnely quietly, "along with thirty pounds of a new powerful plastic explosive and all sorts of fuses."

I had nothing to say except prayers and I kept them to myself.

166

The tall, thin black-cloaked figure emerged on the roof an hour later. By then Donnely had made arrangements with a private detective firm he had kept on retainer for just such a contingency. The burglar carefully relocked the loft and made his way to the edge of the roof. His descent took over a minute. At one point the compressed air-vacuum device, which Alfred said provided the power to make the suction support his weight, gave out on the burglar's right leg. He almost fell. Almost. If it would have been me, I would have panicked and fallen the three stories to the ground. But it wasn't me up there; it was Gabin. He kept his cool and made the descent using only his left leg and arms. Three feet before he came level with the top of the fence, he gathered himself into a tight ball, paused for a second, then shot his body off the bricks with his powerful legs. His body easily cleared the top of the fence. He tucked himself into a neat back flip and landed on the boardlike device in an easy crouch. He retrieved his pole, picked up the boardlike device and vanished into the shadows. One of the cameras picked him up three blocks away as he climbed into an ancient Volkswagen with Illinois plates.

"A small air mattress," Larry whispered approvingly to me as Donnely quietly radioed instructions to the waiting detectives. 'The board thing was a small mattress. He used it as a pad to break his fall. Incredible.'"

Yeah, I thought, incredible. Fantastic. And he's not on our side. I didn't know it then, but two hours later three drum brothers lost control of a car they had recently liberated and took it for a swim in the Chicago River. When the locks on the car doors jammed, they got to conduct a very interesting experiment, discovering that that car model has only enough air in the passenger compartment to last three large hysterical men forty-five minutes. Gabin was a very busy boy.

Donnely called off the private detectives after they verified Gabin was more than three miles away. He had them hold positions close to the factory so they would augment our cameras and tell us if Gabin doubled back to check his work. Of course, they weren't needed, but Donnely didn't know that then. He turned to Larry and said, "Let's go check what our friend has wrought. Jack, you and Alfred stay here. If we don't come back or if anything goes wrong, there are instructions in my top desk drawer at the G. Orevidal residence."

The three hours Larry and Donnely spent inside that factory took years out of my life. Alfred kept trying to reassure me, but his nervousness came through loud and clear. It was almost dawn by the time they returned.

"The man is a true artist," muttered Larry respectfully as he wearily slumped down beside Alfred. "A true artist. He avoided all our security. Of course, I don't think he could get by the real stuff we have at G. Orevidal, but that factory is tighter than almost all government and private 'secure' buildings. After getting in, our boy goes to the basement and uses about ten of that thirty pounds of plastic explosive around the key architectural beams and stress points. He wires that ten pounds into another five pounds he molds around the key corner pipe in the gas system. The first ten pounds might be enough to do the job. The blast would probably weaken the building and make it collapse. But the kicker is the stuff around the gas pipe. That plastic is mixed in with some incendiary devices which will go off a split second before all the other plastic. That will ignite the gas, triple the plastic explosion and mask the whole operation so it looks like a big accidental gas mishap. The concussion will rip that old factory apart like a match box, then suck it down into the hole like a crushed Dixie cup. If that ain't enough, just to be extra-special safe, just to take care of the billion-to-one possibility that maybe, in the split second before the whole building collapses, somebody in the fake living quarters will survive, realize what has happened, don a Buck Rogers flying belt and escape through a window, our boy spreads fifteen pounds of plastic icing coordinated with the basement batch through the attic crawl space. When that blows, the ceiling will turn into shrapnel and anything in the living quarters not in a suit of armor will be sliced to ribbons. If you're in a suit of armor, you won't be able to move fast enough to get out of the upstairs before the downstairs explosion takes the floor away from you. All three sets of plastic are wired to radio time detonators. Gabin can sit ten, maybe twenty miles away, hit the right code sequence, radio instructions to the factory and set the bombs for anywhere from ten seconds to two hours. Neat, clean, simple, quick and totally effective. He's a real artist."

"But we got him, right?" I exclaimed to Donnely. "We got him! You fixed the bombs and they won't go off, right? Right?"

The smile faded from my face as Donnely spoke. "Not exactly," he said. "We left everything intact. Larry altered the detonating devices with Alfred's override controls. We can monitor when Gabin gives the detonation signal, deduce the time element and kick in an additional five-minute delay. That's as far as we dare take it."

"But what are we going to do? The factory is still wired!"

"But he found it!" whispered Donnely excitedly. His composure slipped a little. The tension was beginning to tell on him at this stage. "And he took it! He bought it! Don't you see?"

"What I don't see is what we're going to do!"

Donnely looked at me for a very long time. I saw many things pass over his normally impassive poker face. It finally resolved itself into a firm, commanding, fatherly concern. "What you're going to do," he said quietly, "is quit worrying unnecessarily. The Plan will take care of everything. And the other thing you're going to do is get out to O'Hare. You've got to catch your plane back to Arizona. The big curtain begins its slow rise today."

I grabbed a few hours' sleep on the plane. Day 38 began slightly later than 9 A.M. at Apollo's Hamilton, Arizona, headquarters. After a particularly stunning victory by Edward, who had given up and graciously tried to win our chess matches, I let it slip that something "extremely big" was brewing for Apollo. That afternoon, after Wally's intelligence had confirmed our predictions that Edward would pass the information on to Sebek, I mentioned to my secretary that "Chicago is going to be the biggest thing Apollo and us have ever tried." I swear his ears burned and his eyes lit up. He had no idea anything was happening in Chicago.

Before I went to work the next day, Reginald made me up and carefully drilled me once more. I walked into work looking as if I had spent all night being beaten by a gang of professional thugs who never left physical marks. I actually was haggard and tired, since I hadn't slept well the night before and I was still tired from my Chicago trip. I never sleep well the night before a big operation, but that lack of rest must burn off all my nerves, because I manage to make it through most maneuvers without completely breaking down. Over a cup of coffee I let Edward ask me what was wrong.

I looked at him slowly, searchingly, as a man does to his confidant just before confession. "Edward," I said somewhat truthfully, "let me tell you something. The next few days are going to be the most important in the history of the company. We have an operation going in Chicago which will make everything, and I do mean *everything*, we have done before look like chicken feed. It will be the most profitable deal ever pulled off in American history, and when it is over, our Group's position and that of Apollo's will be unassailable. *Unassailable*." I repeated that word so the pocket tape recorder he carried would be sure to pick it up; then I continued.

"Of course, we're by no means sure we can go through with it. By no means. The only bad thing that could happen, however, would be that some other group would beat us to the punch. Hell, Apollo could go down the drain tomorrow, and everything would still be the same. We could lose control of Apollo, and unless the group that took over Apollo stopped us on this deal or beat us to the punch, they'd be worse off than us. If somebody beats us to this thing, not only do they have Apollo, but they have the most powerful, profitable thing in the country next to the government and the Syndicate. And they'll be close on the heels of them."

With those tantalizing remarks, I drained my cup, left

170

Apollo headquarters for the airport and flew to Chicago, where most of The Group were assembled and waiting. For some reason The Plan called for me to avoid them until after it was all over. Donnely had me check into the Palmer House under an assumed name.

While I was winging my way to Chicago, Edward was rifling my files. The only thing he found which was "unusual" was a bill from some carpenters for some work he hadn't known about. The bill, one of Meredith's best forgeries, was postdated three months. Edward puzzled over that bill for a long time before his Ivy-covered mind finally pieced together what the carpenters had built. He concentrated so hard he didn't notice that the old man washing the outside of the windows was taking an awfully long time to finish his work. Edward probably wouldn't have noticed that the man was slow since Edward had never washed any windows. He also wouldn't have recognized the man, for Reginald, as usual, was in perfect character. When it dawned on Edward that the carpenters had built a "secret cabinet" somewhere in the office, Reginald was wetting the windows for a third time.

It didn't take Edward long to find the secret cabinet, partially because the plot of the movie he had seen with that heiress in her private projection studio the night before had contained the same type of hiding place. The heiress and Edward had been introduced by Raoul (who promised great things to the young lady if she would help him entertain Edward in a special way) and the film had been provided by Reginald. He had a minor part in the movie as a butler who didn't do it.

Inside the secret cabinet, which Larry and Alfred had installed the week before, Edward found a mass of documents. There were cost projection sheets drawn up just the way they do in grad school, profit margin discussions, records of funds shuffling across the country, vague contingency plans, genuine bills of sale from the building of the fake Chicago warehouse and a very cryptic, very important memo from Donnely to me. Edward didn't even stop to consider that

171

Donnely never wrote me memos. When he wants to tell me something, he tells me. The memo was a gem. The Professor, Donnely and I spent a whole day getting it just right:

JACK—

The only thing left for the Chicago Project is to make sure we, in our own names, own the warehouse and all its contents. The Prof says it is absolutely essential that the bill of sale notes we own and claim all responsibility for the contents of the warehouse and states we have inspected all of them. Of course, we don't have to do that until afterward, but the Prof says that legally it is necessary to wrap this thing up tight. In order to keep things under wrap, the inventory list is in code. Alfred says the old man who owns everything now is still anxious to sell, but he's a little crazy. He will negotiate only with the people who will actually be the owners. He's set up two meetings to receive bids. Since we're the only ones who know about the deal (the old man still thinks someone else does), I figure we should skip the first meeting so we can drive the price down when he thinks he doesn't have any buyers besides us. Since we're the only ones who know, no one could show up at the first meeting and talk him into an immediate sale then so we wouldn't have a chance to outbid them. I estimate it will cost us about a million, cash or easily negotiable securities. He insists on COD for the bill of sale. The first meeting is for 10 A.M. [The next day's date was listed.] The one we should show at is set for 2 that afternoon. If I can't make it, you'll have to go. You'll recognize him because he'll have a red rose in his lapel and will be carrying a copy of *The Complete Sherlock Holmes*. His real name is Signatio Marchetti. The code phrase will be "Professor Moriarty, I presume," and he will reply, "Gazeebo to you." You'll meet him in the basement bathroom of Chicago's City Hall. He says to use the front entrance by the Picasso. After the transaction all we have to do is show up at the warehouse that night and take personal possession of the goods until the old man files the papers

172

of transition the next morning. Then we've done it! I figure this should make us the biggest, richest group in the country, if not the world. The Arabs better move over. If you still want to buy Vermont, I'll make up the few million you'll be short (ha-ha!).

DAN

Right after Edward read that memo, he left work, took a taxi to the airport and caught a shuttle plane to Phoenix and the headquarters of Sebek and company. He didn't notice a fruit picker in a rented pickup following him to make sure he got to the airport, but then Reginald is a fruit picker's fruit picker. As Edward's plane took off, Reginald made two calls, one to Raoul waiting in the Phoenix airport and one to Donnely waiting in Chicago. Then Reginald hopped into one of two Lear jets rented secretly by Donnely and was flown to Chicago.

Raoul trailed Edward from the airport to Sebek's headquarters. Edward didn't notice that one of the pilfered file folders he carried had a thick backing. In that backing was the smallest transmitter Alfred and Larry could make. The only trouble Raoul had trailing Edward came when their car radio played Percy Sledge's "When a Man Loves a Woman" and he got so involved in the music's tight rhythm he almost missed a turn. When I think of Meredith, I can understand how he felt. Raoul listened gleefully to the transmitted dialogue as Rosale and Valentine deduced exactly what we wanted them to deduce from the files Edward brought them. That, coupled with his reports of our "strange" behavior as of late, convinced them we were on the trail of something big. The memo was the clincher, for it told them how they could capitalize on our work and wipe us out at the same time. All they had to do was beat us on the deal by showing up for the first bid session the next morning. Rosale and Valentine sent Edward back to mind the Apollo headquarters, then left on the run in order to catch a flight to Chicago.

At eleven-thirty that night, Raoul broke into the offices of Sebek, Inc. He had no trouble foiling their security. He

173

planted carefully drawn-up receipts, bills of sale, memos and other documents showing that Sebek Industries had owned and developed the merchandise in the Chicago warehouses all along. He even planted the code book for the inventory sheets. He then flew to Chicago in the other rented jet.

Right now you are probably wondering how, even with all this preparation, we expected two sharp men like Rosale and Valentine to fall for the Chicago deal. The answer is simple. We made the Chicago deal seem like a natural extension of everything that had happened, and they greedily didn't stop to question what kind of pebble was making what kind of ripples in the pond. By not doing that, they allowed us to enter their power sphere and move them through a sphere of neutrality into our sphere of power. We also didn't give them a lot of time to find other options. As long as we didn't trip up and as long as we used their force to defeat itself, we would be OK. As long as we didn't trip up. Or nobody threw a stray pebble.

What, you may also ask, was the Chicago deal? The answer is simple: There was no Chicago deal. Like Apollo in the beginning, the deal existed only on paper. The Chicago deal was a setup. Donnely filled the fake warehouse with various types of contraband, contraband which was so illegal and unmarketable that no attorney save the Professor could get its owner out of a very stiff conviction. That was the contraband which Sebek, Inc. (Rosale and Valentine), would buy and possess the next morning, the contraband which their records in Phoenix showed they had possessed and controlled for some time. What kind of contraband? A ton of contaminated heroin, famous paintings stolen from influential people and museums all over the world, poorly counterfeited money, marked stolen money from various banks, false gas ration coupons, a monogrammed purse snatched from the wife of a Machine-supported Chicago alderman, bootlegged gambling devices not approved of by Wally Kearns' "former associates," stolen inoperable U.S. military equipment (including five hundred thirty-eight portable chemical latrines, two jeeps and a tank), clumsily forged

174

welfare identification cards, forged out-of-date Wall Street certificates—in short, white elephants of crime which fences employed by Wally's "former associates" had been unable to unload. The owners of such merchandise were guilty of interstate transportation of stolen property, possession of the same, counterfeiting, drug trafficking, several robbery felonies, several counts of profit-related violence, and, of course, income-tax evasion. All that lovely contraband cost The Group a mere half million dollars because it constituted a white elephant, a plague-carrying white elephant which Rosale and Valentine were hurrying to Chicago to buy for one million dollars.

But how would such a transaction help rid The Group of its problems with Sebek, Gabin and the Tom Toms? Ah, that comes later.

The Pull-Off

It was a beautiful Chicago spring morning. The smog lifted and clear blue sky peeked out from behind the John Hancock Building. The Wrigley Building even looked like slightly dirty white walls instead of slightly white dirty walls. And Picasso's squat statue presided over the city from its roost in front of City Hall. I spent a lot of time that morning trying to name the creature it resembled most. I finally decided it was a praying mantis poised for attack.

Everything was ready. One of Wally's "former associates" who could be rented for the paltry sum of ten thousand dollars had arranged a meeting with a frustrated crusading U.S. attorney to tell him about a huge shipment of contraband moving into the Chicago area that night. The meeting was scheduled for the City Hall plaza, where the stoolie would point out the major participants in the transaction to the U.S. attorney.

At 9:50 Reginald, disguised so even I barely recognized him, checked the red rose in his lapel, shifted his copy (the same one Donnely stole from the Marines) of *Sherlock Holmes* so the title could be read, subsumed himself into his character and entered City Hall. Five minutes later a limousine deposited Rosale, Valentine and their hired bodyguard, Bruno. Bruno stayed outside City Hall, walking around the plaza talking to the pigeons while his employers scurried to keep their appointment. Neither Bruno nor the chauffeur paid much attention to the punk who sauntered by the limousine, tripped over a tin can, stumbled and fell against the back of the car. They watched him to make sure he wasn't an adversary, but the only people they expected trouble from were the Tom Toms, and the punk looked too rational to be a drum brother. They didn't see Raoul slap the small glob of sticky plastic on the bottom right corner of the limousine's rear window. The plastic contained a special bug developed by Alfred and Larry which was so sensitive it could use the window as a sounding board and transmit the discussions in the rear seat for a distance of almost three miles. I carried the receiver disguised as a transistor radio, complete with earplugs, snugly riding in my ear. His mission accomplished, Raoul caught a bus for the G. Orevidal residence.

I would have loved to have watched the "Marchetti"-Sebek meeting, but we didn't want to crowd things. I can only say that Reginald must have given the performance of a lifetime, for at 10:19 he strolled from the building carrying a suitcase containing one million dollars in easily negotiable paper. He assumed another character before he reached the bus stop. Five minutes later Kearns and Valentine ecstatically emerged. They didn't notice the stoolie and a startled U.S. attorney watching their progress. The U.S. attorney, knowing no one at his headquarters would believe that Rosale and Valentine were working together on something and that they were guarded by the infamous Bruno, commandeered a roll of film from a beautiful, charming, talented, intelligent black woman who happened to snap several pictures of some pigeons walking behind the suspicious trio. Her pictures would naturally show the three men. The woman gave the U.S. attorney a false name and address to mail the remuneration to before she drove off in a taxi. Meredith was great.

Rosale, Valentine and Bruno piled into their limousine. Bruno sat in the front. I barely heard him grunt commands to the driver, but Rosale and Valentine came in loud and clear. I'll omit their laughter, congratulatory exclamations and general enthusiasm and merely report the more important words I heard before the static became too great and they faded away:

ROSALE: We did it! We did it! We scuttled them! Now all we have left is those idiot Tom Toms and our friend Gabin.

VALENTINE: We're not through yet. Donnely is no fool. He'll figure out what we've done and I'm betting he'll come after us. If not now, very soon. We gotta provide for that.

ROSALE [after a pause]: You're right, of course. Such a pity, too. At some point in the future they might have again stumbled on to something profitable we could use. Ah, well. Do you have the radio unit Gabin gave you?

[GABIN's words were barely intelligible, so I'm guessing on some of the things he said.]

ROSALE [after raising GABIN on a small walkie-talkie-like radio]: My associate and I have come to the conclusion that it would be best if you proceed with your primary task as quickly as possible.

GABIN: Is there any special reason for this sudden reversal in policy?

VALENTINE [shouting so he could be heard on the radio held by ROSALE]: Naw, we just decided you should move on this now. As soon as you can. No special reason. Then finish up with that other little chore and you're through.

GABIN: How is your business progressing?

ROSALE: The deal fell apart.

VALENTINE: Look, Gabin, all you have to worry about is your end. Waste 'em.

At that point the limousine must have turned behind a building, for the transmission went dead.

I felt as though a butcher I had been carefully watching to avoid being cheated had suddenly gone crazy and was chopping me up with a meat cleaver, freezing me with pain, numbing my mind with terror. Rosale and Valentine were slashing The Plan to ribbons. Gabin was moving on us out of schedule. And I was the only one who knew. The only reason we had bugged the limousine at all was to gather followup intelligence after Sebek took the hook. They took the hook all right, but The Plan caught more than we bargained for.

Meredith, Donnely and the others were safe at the G. Orevidal residence, waiting for me to join them and enjoy the exultation of victory. At least they were safe for the time being. Gabin had been loosed; the falcon had been flung. I had seen him operate: I knew it was only a matter of time before he spotted his correct prey and swooped for the kill. I stood there in the plaza square, immobilized by the sickening vision of huge talons embedded in my screaming, defenseless Meredith's back. Then I ran for a pay phone booth across the street.

The phone company hadn't got around to replacing the old-fashioned glass-enclosed booth with the new exposed open-air phone column. The booth door stuck. I wasted ten precious seconds getting inside and shutting the door. I noticed it as I was slapping my pockets for change.

You've seen it dozens of times. Abstract art prints which suddenly unravel into scenes of horses playing in the fields. A psychological visual diagram which, when you stare at it, constantly shifts: One second it's a goblet; the next second it's two profiles facing each other. A forest scene in which you suddenly realize there's a fawn standing perfectly still against the hodgepodge of color. It's an image blending in and out of its surroundings. You see it; then you don't; then it's back again always changing, switching before your senses and mind have a chance to decide what it *really* is. The image I saw that day shimmered amid the busy Chicago street scene. In an alleyway across the street, evidently unseen by the milling crowds, a tall, thin blond man in a trench coat seemed to be pointing his extended right arm at me. The hand on the end of his arm looked funny, black, long, skinny. The scene kept changing through those few seconds while I foolishly concentrated most of my mind on the search for dimes. Before I found the coins or had a chance to decide what the image really was, it removed all doubt of its identity by sending a bullet through the glass not six inches from my head.

There are three time-places I always feel terrified, trapped and helpless. One is while in a public toilet stall while relieving myself, my pants around my ankles. Another is when I'm at home alone in the shower with the water going full blast deadening my hearing, the steam rising to obscure my vision and memories of *Psycho* dancing through my head. The third place is an exposed glass telephone booth with the door

179

firmly shut and a man standing across the street calmly firing rounds at me with his silenced revolver. The feeling in the third instance goes beyond terror when my assailant is Gabin, and I am trapped tighter than any snared rabbit.

My mind shifted directly from terror to calm contemplation without pausing at panic. I did not question that I was definitely trapped and being shot at by Gabin. Glass crinkled, two more holes appeared in the phone booth above my ridiculously crouched form, and my second thought noted that he had missed again. Redundancy I admit to, but clarity I claim. From there Donnely-trained logic and experience took over. Gabin, the best assassin money can buy, was less than thirty yards away shooting at a basically immobile target in broad daylight and he had missed three times. That didn't make sense; *ergo*, something was wrong with the formula's composition. Gabin did not miss, especially in those circumstances. Consider: He was there, he was who he was, he was shooting, and none of the bullets had hit me. That meant he was on target, which meant he was not trying to hit me with those bullets, which didn't make sense, because I had just heard our friends of Sebek give him explicit instructions to waste The Group and I was part of The Group.

That's when it came to me. I was *part* of The Group. He was after all of us. Since almost no time had elapsed between his receiving the order and his commencement of the order's execution, it was logical to assume he hadn't needed to "find" me, that he had been right on top of me for some time, probably from the time I landed in Chicago the day before. Why was he shooting at me then? Simple, I thought as I finally forced open the door and rolled behind a parked car. Another bullet whizzed by me to flatten a delivery truck tire. Bystanders were beginning to note my rather peculiar behavior, but Chicago is a tough town used to peculiar behavior. Gabin was using a variation on the old hunting technique of flushing his quarry. He knew that if I were attacked, my obvious reaction would be to seek the safest place I could find. That place would be The Group's secret rathole. After I reached "safety" the logical thing for me to do would be to rally the rest of The Group to safety, too. Then he would have us all, one neat, tidy little package, tied up nicely and waiting for him to deliver us while we sat foolishly assured of the safety of our rathole. It was an absolutely beautiful plan. I knew Gabin would make it work, too. And I knew I couldn't let him, for if Gabin succeeded, Meredith and the others would die.

There was only one possible solution. I had to lead him to the wrong rathole, diverting his attention, buying time for The Group to find out The Plan had gone wrong and develop new alternatives, and hope somehow to survive. I resigned myself to personal failure on the last portion of that solution. But in a way I was lucky, at least as far as my idea went. I knew the logical thing to do was take Gabin to the wrong rathole he already thought was the right rathole. I had to lead him to the factory.

I didn't figure he would need any more help from me, so I didn't make it easy for him. I ran.

Women thrust baby buggies in front of me as obstacles. I hurdled them. Fat construction workers rose up to block me. I knocked them down. A blurry cop tried to restrain my flight. I left him wallowing in my wake. Mercifully Alfred's old pickup started on the first try. I left a peel of rubber on the street, wiping out a Corvette as I shot out of the parking place and tore down the street to the expressway. Noon rush hour. I passed cars at seventy-five mph, weaving from the far right to the far left lanes. I took the lakeshore S curve designed for thirty mph at fifty-five, sideswiping a chicken farm truck. It tipped over, scattering frantic birds all over the expressway. I kept going. In my rearview mirror I saw other vehicles plow into the pileup.

Four blocks from the factory I realized something else was wrong. The factory was supposed to be deserted, yet more than a dozen cars stood by the main entrance. I slowed my pace to an acceptable rate, ignored the rearview mirror and slowly drove around the corner to the side entrance. Just before I turned the corner, two men emerged from the factory's main entrance to take up positions on each side of the

181

door. One of the men, a black, wore the suede jacket and red pointed cap of the Spiritual and Revolutionary Brotherhood of Tom Toms. The other was a husky white man in a hard hat. I couldn't tell for sure, but I was betting the stickers on his hat showed he belonged to the United Laborers and Workers Union. All of which didn't make sense and further went to show how far The Plan had collapsed: We intended for Rosale and Valentine to show up that night so our frustrated crusading U.S. attorney could act on his hot tip and bust them *flagrante delicto,* sending them with massive sentences to prison, where Wally guaranteed they would be assigned to the cloutless crowd. We had definitely not intended for the Tom Toms to be anywhere around. In a way I wasn't surprised to see the union boys and drum brothers: Everything else had gone so wrong it was almost right that they were there. I wasn't sure how their presence affected my plan to make Gabin think this was the right rathole. I didn't have time to consider all such ramifications. Hoping that my momentum would suck Gabin behind me and that somehow I could still pull a miracle out of the situation, I dashed through a side gate, climbed the fire escape to what would have been the second-floor landing and quietly eased my way through an emergency exit trapdoor leading to an open crawlway encircling the factory's floor. I gently shut the trapdoor behind me, but I left it unlocked.

Even in hanging-droplight-augmented daylight the "warehouse"-factory was dark, musty. I made my way to a loading dock jutting out over the factory floor and slouched down behind some cartons of dull, "dirty" 1950ish court-banned blue movies which were still technically "illegal" and were also so tame they would cause no ripples in Bicentennial Peoria and were hence unmarketable anywhere. I looked back toward the trapdoor in time to see it gently close again. I *felt* rather than saw I had a companion on the catwalk. I closed my eyes and tried to think of some pleasant last thoughts, but my immediate environment was too overpowering. The warehouse smelled of dust, machine oil and human sweat. Some of the last odor was left over from the efforts of The

182

Group when we unloaded the merchandise. Some of it came from the shouting men standing on the main floor below my hiding place. A lot of it came from my nervous body.

John H1, John H9, Bruno, Valentine and Rosale were all yelling at the same time. They stood warily in the center of the main floor. Drum brothers, union members and some of Rosale's special junior executives ringed the shouters. John H9 carried his unsheathed bolo knife and Bruno kept tapping his hand with his lead-weighted baseball bat. I could feel Gabin, but I still couldn't see him.

It seems that the drum brothers wanted a piece of the action, a rather large piece from the way John H1 was screaming. It also seems that Sebek and associates did not particularly want to part with any of their newly acquired pie. This meant no one had examined the contents of any of the boxes standing around the room. I kept nervously glancing over my shoulder as I listened to our former associates scream at each other.

"All I know is," shouted John H1, "the brothers have been poppin' off lately in a lot bigger numbers than our great shining destiny designates! The coincidence between that happening and you guys all of a sudden striking it rich by taking this bundle away from Donnely just when we, the wave of the future, were about to consider another transitional alliance with you and your reactionary forces is just too great for my eyes to countenance!"

"Listen to me, you silly son of a bitch!" interrupted the Sweetheart of organized labor in less than loving tones. "I don't care what you think! This here is our property and you get your goons out and off it before the boys and I. . . ."

"Gentlemen, gentlemen," moderated diplomatic Chamber of Commerce President Rosale. "Please. This is getting us nowhere. If nothing else, all this commotion might damage these precious goods; then all would lose.

"Now as I see it, we can all work together. Mr. H1 feels grossly aggrieved that he was not able to contact us about an alliance before Mr. Valentine and myself were able to initiate this lucrative transaction. I can also understand Mr. H1's dis-

183

may at the rather alarming losses his congregation has been suffering lately. While I do not benefit from sources such as the anonymous caller who phoned him and told him of his interest which led to our meeting accidentally here today, I also have what he would call street ears. These sources tell me that indeed there is a plot to destroy the Tom Toms. But my ears rightly pin the blame where it belongs, on Donnely."

All our former associates stared at each other while Rosale paused.

"That's correct," he continued. "Donnely. He hired a man called Gabin to eliminate you and your organization. I believe he also has designs on Mr. Valentine and myself. Now I happen to know a good deal about this Mr. Gabin, including how he can be found. Because I am shocked by the calamities which Donnely is inflicting on your organization, and because I fear for Mr. Valentine and my own situation if this Gabin and this Donnely are not stopped, I think Mr. Valentine will go along with my offer of, say, nine percent of the gross of this warehouse to you as well as what assistance we can render you if you help yourselves and us by eliminating Gabin, Donnely and the others."

While the drum brothers quietly discussed the latest explanation-offer of events, Rosale turned to his stunned colleague and said, "It's the only reasonable, practical solution. It also helps us with our . . . consultant problem, to say nothing of taking care of Donnely and his lackey Gabin. It's the time and the place."

Phil the Sweetheart frowned, shrugged and said, "Why not?"

"The Spiritual and Revolutionary Brotherhood of the Tom Toms considers your offer," announced John H1 solemnly, "and while agreeing in spirit, we beg to differ on the small points. We want fifty percent."

"Preposterous!" shouted Rosale. "Even if you had been in on this from the beginning, even if we weren't doing you a favor by helping you get Gabin and Donnely off your backs, you wouldn't be worth even twelve percent!"

"Easily forty!" retorted John H1.

184

"You ain't worth nothing more than eighteen percent!" chimed in Phil the Sweetheart.

As the conversation again degenerated into general shouting, I thought I saw a flash of light from the trapdoor opening, a figure slipping out, then the trapdoor shutting. Halfway through that process I shifted slightly to get a better look. I suddenly remembered the building was wired, and it was logical to assume the electrician had just left to flip the switch. Before I had a chance to consider the matter further, the rotten wooden floor collapsed underneath me, dropping my startled form to the warehouse floor and scaring the hell out of our former associates.

I landed on a bundle of stolen precious silks and carpets which had been rendered unmarketable when the thief's camel urinated on them. The bundle bounced me up like a trampoline, and Lady Luck, who must have been the one who threw my pebble through the floor, landed me on my feet. The shouting had ceased the instant the floor gave way. Now all eyes silently riveted on me.

What could I do? I waved. And then ran like hell.

"Get him!" screamed John H1, Harold Rosale and Sweetheart Phil Valentine, a chorus singing in agreement for the first time that day. With Bruno and John H9 in the lead, their employees and associates gave chase.

Errol Flynn would have been proud of me that day. I jumped, dodged, weaved and ran, evading hordes of villains for at least ten minutes. Around and around the warehouse we flew. But like in the movies, the reels do change. I decided I shouldn't be completely exhausted when they finally caught me (as I knew they eventually would) so right under the second-floor loading dock through which I had fallen, I stopped, pivoted and faced my adversaries. That unexpected action froze them in their tracks, but only momentarily. Then slowly, surely, John H9 and Bruno advanced, spreading out until Bruno was on my right and John H9 was on my left.

There are some sounds you never forget, sounds you can immediately identify: a crying baby, a barking dog, the blare of a car horn. At that instant I heard a sound that I knew no matter how hard I tried, I could never forget or mistake after the first time I heard it: machine-gun fire.

True, the stuttering, crackling coughs from the Ingram machine pistols lack the deep, full-bodied roar of the heavy machine guns I heard in Vietnam, but there is no mistaking the basic source. I hit the deck as quickly and as instinctively as all the others who had also evidently heard that sound before. Bullets whistled far above our heads to bounce off the opposite wall. Yes, bounce: Larry and Alfred altered stolen riot-control rubber bullets for the 9mm Ingrams. A few rubber slugs ricocheted and broke the overhead lights, but no one was hurt.

The bugle that usually signals the arrival of the emancipating cavalry wasn't there, but we had music. Bass chords of the Rolling Stones' "Street Fighting Man" blared from the transistor radio strapped to Raoul's hip. As the Stones started the second verse, Donnely's scream jerked me to my feet while my confused companions on the warehouse floor scurried for cover. "Jack!" he yelled from the second-floor trapdoor. "Hurry! The override is running out!" Then he and Raoul slapped fresh ammunition clips in their weapons and fired from the catwalk to the warehouse floor, spraying the entire area with their rebounding arsenal. Panicked and bewildered, drum brothers, union members and businessmen huddled behind boxes of contraband and tried to gather their wits while I dashed up a ladder twice as quickly as I had once run through elephant grass. Donnely hosed the warehouse down with a third clip while Raoul and I scurried down the outside fire escape. By the time Donnely slammed the door the men inside had regained enough composure to return our fire. Their bullets were not rubber. Several tore through the trapdoor as Donnely slammed it shut and a wood splinter sliced his cheek. He ignored the blood, slid down the railing; then the three of us ran through the side gate. As our feet touched the opposite curb, Meredith appeared in the back of an open furniture van halfway down the block to scream, "Hit it!" We flew through the air, diving

186

to the ground like Olympic swimmers tearing into the finals for a gold medal. The concrete and clay smashed us harder than any cold-water belly flop and felt better than any warm shower. I barely had time to fling my arms over my head in approved Marine fashion.

KKKaaBOOOOMMMMMN!

The ground shuddered and I thought of Hemingway. When the pebble shower ceased, we climbed to our feet. Behind us the dust cloud was still rising. The putrid stench of gas filled the air. A very large hole grew where once had stood an old factory, fake warehouse, fake rathole full of contraband, union members, drum brothers, aspiring corporate tycoons and Bruno, former bodyguard to Syndicate gangster Wallace Kearns. Sirens wailed in the distance and from the tenement apartment building across the street I heard a radio playing Joan Baez's "Amazing Grace." Donnely plucked at my sleeve, turning me around. As we limply shuffled to the van, he jabbered at me almost incoherently.

"I had to do it this way, Jack, I had to! I'm sorry, I'm sorry! But Gabin was too good! We had to give him more than the fake rathole! We had to give him a fake rat, too! One that was so good Gabin couldn't smell the scam on him. We had to give him a fake rat who thought he was real. We had to give him you!"

"Then he was on me all along?" I said, slowing down slightly. Somehow I had pulled a leg muscle.

"No, no, no, just for the last few days and some of the times when you were out getting stuff. I knew the rest of us stood a better chance of sliding by him and doing what we had to do if we let him latch onto the most essential member of The Group."

Raoul had fallen on his radio in the dive, breaking it and bruising his hip. I helped him into the back of the van. The few people running by us were too busy gawking at the explosion site to pay us any mind. "Then the explosion, Rosale, Valentine, John H1, John H9, all the others, you planned that?"

"No," said Donnely as he threw the machine pistol up to

Larry. "It was one of many possibilities. When we found out Gabin was on you—Larry had you under surveillance since you hit Chicago—and Rosale and Valentine were headed to the warehouse, I had Meredith tip the Tom Toms. If Gabin hadn't followed you, then come out and set the fuse like he did, we would have released the knockout gas in the warehouse and figured something else out, maybe leaving them all there for the U.S. attorney to find. Remember, we kept track of the whole show through the bugs, security cameras and bomb monitors."

"Then we're through," I said as I gingerly hopped up to sit on the truck bed. I looked at my lovely Meredith, who leaned against the truck wall. She was drained, almost sallow, nerve-racked. And relieved, very, very relieved. "It's over. The Plan's done."

Donnely looked up at me grimly. "No, not quite. There's one thing left. There's still Gabin."

I looked down at the lanky, scuffed-up man I knew so well and so little. The blood from the cut on his head trickled down past the bags under his eyes; a thin red stream zig-zagged across his pale skin. His voice seemed calmer and he had stopped shaking, but I asked anyway.

"Are you all right?"

"Are *you?*" he replied. Then he smiled slightly.

Meredith lightly touched my left shoulder and I reached up to grasp her hand. "Sure," I said, "with her, you and the others, I got it all."

"Then I'm OK, too," he said. He turned and slowly walked away. He stopped on the edge of the crowd and stood there, waiting. Meredith squeezed my hand tightly. I tried to reassure her with a smile. I looked up over my right shoulder and saw a tight-lipped street fighter named Raoul. Hidden under his rain poncho so none of the gathering crowd could see was another Ingram machine pistol. This one had real bullets. Alfred sat farther back in the truck, carefully twisting the knobs on the receiving set to pick up the noise coming from the bug Donnely carried in his right jean jacket pocket. Larry carefully watched the radio, ready to replace instantly

188

any tube which might blow. I could see the back of Reginald's head through the window connecting the cargo compartment with the driver's section. The Professor sat to his right in the passenger seat.

He came from out of nowhere, sliding easily through the crowd until he stood next to Donnely. The two of them watched the mass of confusion as policemen, civil defense workers, power company troubleshooters and firemen converged on the factory site along with hundreds of curious, milling neighborhood residents. His hair was blond that day and he wore the tan trench coat. I watched his back. The two of them stood silently for several minutes. A policeman passed in front of them. He stopped to ask if they knew anything about what had happened. Donnely said no. He also declined the cop's halfhearted offer to send him to the aid station for treatment of his cut.

"Awfully big hole, isn't it!" Gabin's fine, smooth words came as the cop disappeared in the crowd.

"Much bigger than most people would have anticipated," replied Donnely solemnly.

"Indeed. Had you anticipated it?"

"There was always that possibility."

"It could have turned out much differently. You could have hit us with the gas."

I heard Donnely smile. "Not if you knew about it."

Gabin laughed. "Quite right, quite right. I was ready. I wasn't sure about the rathole, so I went in to look again. I was completely ready for you, but I hadn't expected my . . . former employers to be quite so perverse in their perfidy. A mistake on my part."

I saw Donnely shrug. "Perhaps. It didn't catch you, and everyone makes them. But they weren't really your employers. You know that. They tried to use you, not employ you. That's why you activated the plastic."

"You know me quite well, Mr. Donnely. Quite well."

"Well enough to know how your artistic sensibilities feel about being betrayed, swindled. And well enough to trust you now."

"Why? Why trust me now? If things had worked out differently, I would have killed you as part of my job."

"But things work out as they do, not as they might. Not only do you now have no reason to kill us, you can't under your own honor code. In a sense you actually worked for us, and we have paid you by letting you live."

"When was my life yours to pay back?" Gabin's tone showed amusement. I heard Raoul suck in his breath and shift the Ingram under his poncho.

"Perhaps several times in the streets. Definitely in the warehouse. Now."

Gabin paused for a moment before he laughed. "Mr. Donnely, you are incredible. I will not grant you your assumption and the only way I can deny it definitively is to challenge it irrevocably. That I do not wish to do. Just remember your own observation: Things work out as they do, not as they might.

"But you are right. You and your Group have nothing to fear from me. Ever. You may or may not be former employers of mine protected under my honor code. I will not quibble over meaningless definitions. But you most certainly are, like me, true artists. True artists do not compete with each other. There is too little art left in this world for such foolishness. True artists may move in different spheres. When their spheres touch in what could be a volatile way, they pass on by."

Gabin slowly turned until he half faced our truck as well as Donnely. He smiled, bowed slightly, then vanished into the crowd. Donnely stood where he was until the tall blond man had been gone for almost a minute. Donnely slowly walked to the truck, hopped aboard, and we drove away.

The Pushover

We had a strange sort of dinner last week. It wasn't really what you would call a celebration, nor was it a sad dinner or a wake or a formal occasion like a coronation banquet. It was something like parts of all those events, which, of course, it should have been. The dinner was held at the G. Orevidal residence and all The Group were there. We were all tired from the Senate investigation of Apollo, the interviews with the press, the conferences with officials, the fan letters, the whole thing. That afternoon the Chicago *Daily News'* major columnist had announced that the mysterious explosion at the Gary warehouse will probably never be solved. Two separate Associated Press news stories said there are still no clues to the whereabouts of noted businessman and New York Chamber of Commerce President Harold Rosale or famous labor leader and president of the United Laborers and Workers Union Phillip "Phil the Sweetheart" Valentine. Nobody seems to miss John H1, John H9 or Bruno.

The afternoon of the dinner we got a telegram from Wally Kearns. It simply read: INTERESTING.

We didn't reply.

Donnely sat at the head of the table, if a round table can be said to have a head. We had earlier agreed that we all needed a long vacation. We are slowly selling Apollo to some fairly honest and respectable businessmen. We are having trouble finding willing, suitable buyers.

After dessert Donnely slowly stood and raised his glass of champagne. Raoul turned down his new radio and followed suit. Alfred and Larry, wearing dress white lab smocks, stood

191

together, glasses held high. Reginald stood as a star, goblet extended. The Professor trembled slightly as he rose, but it wasn't from standing on his own legs. Meredith and I held hands as we raised glasses with the others.

"Friends," Donnely said, losing the battle to the tears like the rest of us, "here's to our pebbles and ponds!"

It was *excellent* champagne.